THE EMPEROR'S SNUFF-BOX

John Dickson Carr
THE EMPEROR'S SNUFF-BOX

Carroll & Graf Publishers, inc.
New York

Carroll & Graf Publishers, Inc.
260 Fifth Avenue
New York, NY 10001

ISBN 0-7867-0223-0

Manufactured in the United States of America.

THE EMPEROR'S SNUFF-BOX

I

WHEN Eve Neill divorced Ned Atwood, the suit was not contested. And, even though the charge was infidelity with a famous woman tennis-player, it created far less scandal than Eve had expected.

For one thing, they had been married in Paris, at the American Church in the Avenue George Fifth. So a divorce in Paris remained legal in England. Only a line or two found its way into the English press. Eve and Ned had made their home at La Bandelette—"the fillet," that strip of silver beach which in those days of peace was perhaps the most fashionable wateringplace in France — and few ties with London still remained. A comment here, a laugh there, and the matter seemed closed.

But to Eve it seemed more humiliating to divorce than to be divorced.

This, no doubt, was morbid. It was the aftermath of a nerve-strain which had reduced even her easygoing temperament to the edge of hysteria. And then she always had to combat the verdict of the world on her unfortunate appearance.

"My dear," said one woman, "anybody who marries Ned Atwood ought to know what to expect."

"But are you sure," said another, "that the fault's all on one side? Look at her photograph. Just *look* at it!"

Eve at this time was twenty-eight. At nineteen she had inherited the fortune of a Lancashire father with more than a few cotton-mills, and a bursting pride in his daughter. At twenty-five she married Ned Atwood because (a) he was good-looking, (b) she was lonely, and (c) he quite seriously threatened suicide if she refused to marry him.

For a person of rather muddled good-nature and a complete lack of suspicion, Eve resembled the most sinister of heart-breakers. She was slender; she was rather tall; she had a figure which Lebec of the Place Vendôme tricked out into that of Circe. She had light chestnut hair, long and heavy as fleece, done into a style vaguely Edwardian. Her pink-and-white complexion, her gray eyes and half-smiling mouth, added to the illusion. On Frenchmen her effect was especially pronounced. Even the presiding judge, who granted her the divorce, seemed to have some suspicion.

In France, the law rules that before a divorce can be granted the two parties must meet — face to face, in a private interview — as a last effort to see whether their differences may not be adjusted. Eve never forgot that morning in the judge's chambers at Versailles: a warm April morning, full of the magic which used to stir Paris in springtime.

The judge, a kindly fussy man with whiskers, was quite sincere. But he carried on in what seemed a wildly theatrical manner.

"Madame!" he said. "Monsieur! Before it is too late, I implore you to stop and consider!"

As for Ned Atwood . . .

You would have sworn that butter wouldn't melt in Ned's mouth. His famous charm, which radiated from him now and of which Eve herself was conscious, animated the sunny room. It could not be marred even by a hangover. His expression of hurt and appealing penitence inspired confidence. Lighthaired and blue-eyed, eternally youthful though past his middle thirties, he stood by the window as a picture of eager attention. Eve could admit that he was damnably, entanglingly attractive, and it had got him into all his troubles.

"Is there anything," the judge was pursuing, "that I can say of marriage?"

"No," said Eve. "Please!"

"If I could only persuade madame and monsieur to reflect . . ."

"You don't have to persuade me," Ned said huskily. "*I* never wanted this divorce."

The little judge whirled round and seemed to tower.

"Monsieur, be silent! It is you who have offended. It is you who should ask madame's pardon."

"I do," Ned said quickly. "I'll ask it on my knees, if you like."

And he walked towards Eve, while the judge stroked his whiskers and looked hopeful. Ned was attractive. He was also very clever. Eve wondered, with a flick of fear, whether she would ever be free of him.

"The co-respondent in this case," pursued the judge, surreptitiously consulting his notes, "this Madame," he consulted his notes again, "Buhlmeer-Smeeth . . ."

"Eve, she doesn't mean a thing to me! I swear she doesn't!"

Eve spoke wearily.

"Haven't we been over all this before?"

"Betsy Bulmer-Smith," said Ned, "is a cow and a trollop. I can't think what came over me. If you're jealous of her . . ."

"I'm not jealous of her. But you might try burning *her* arm with a lighted cigarette, just out of spite, and see how she likes it."

An expression of helpless and hopeless injury went over Ned's face, like that of a misunderstood small boy.

"You're not holding *that* against me, surely?"

"I'm not holding anything against you, Ned dear. I only want to get this over with. Please!"

"I was drunk. I didn't know what I was doing."

"Ned, let's not argue about it. I told you it didn't matter."

"Then why are you being so unfair to me?"

She was sitting by a big table with an impressive inkstand. Ned put his hand over hers. They had been speaking in English, which the little judge did not understand. He coughed, turned away, and began to exhibit passionate interest in a picture hanging over the bookcase. Eve suddenly wondered, with Ned's hand gripping hers, whether they meant to force her back to Ned in spite of herself.

What Ned said, in a way, was quite true. With all his charm and cleverness, he remained as unconscious of the streak of cruelty in his nature as any small boy.

Cruelty — even the semi-comic "mental" cruelty, which Eve had always despised as a hypocritical half-measure — would have been grounds for divorce. But the charge of adultery was quick and conclusive. It stopped there. It was enough. There were things in her home life with Ned which Eve would have died rather than admit in court.

"Marriage," said the judge, addressing the picture over the bookcase, "is the only happy estate for man and woman."

"Eve," said Ned, "*will* you give me another chance?"

A tame psychologist at a party had once told Eve that she was more susceptible than most persons to the power of suggestion. But she was not quite susceptible enough for this.

Ned's touch left her unmoved and faintly revolted. In his own way Ned really loved her. For a second she was tempted: tempted merely to avoid all this fuss and upset and turmoil by saying yes. But saying "yes" out of weak good nature, saying "yes" just to avoid trouble, wasn't good enough if it meant returning to Ned and Ned's ways and Ned's friends and an existence where you felt you were always living in soiled clothes. Eve didn't know whether to burst out laughing at the judge's whiskers, or break down and weep.

"I'm sorry," she answered, and got up.

The judge swung round with a gleam of hope.

"Madame says . . . ?"

"No. It doesn't march," said Ned.

For a second she had been afraid he would smash

something, in the tantrums he had shown before. But the mood passed, if he had ever had it. He stood looking steadily back at her, jingling coins in his pocket. He smiled, showing strong teeth. Fine little wrinkles deepened at the corners of his eyes.

"You're still in love with me, you know," he stated, with a strength of naïveté which showed he really believed it.

Eve picked up her handbag from the table.

"And, what's more, I'm going to prove it to you," he added. Seeing her look, his smile deepened. "Oh, not now! You must have time to cool down; or maybe I mean warm up. I'm going abroad for a while. But when I come back . . ."

He did not come back.

Determined to outface the neighbors, but living in fear of what they might be saying, Eve settled down at La Bandelette. She need not have worried. Nobody troubled about what went on at the Villa Miramar, rue des Anges. Over watering-places like La Bandelette — which lived for its brief social season, and for the English and American visitors who lost money at its Casino — reigned a vacuum of curiosity. Eve Neill knew nobody in the rue des Anges; and nobody knew her.

Throughout spring deepening into summer, the

crowds shifted in La Bandelette. Its queerly gabled and painted houses made it resemble a town in a Walt Disney film. The pine-scented air was aromatic; open carriages clopped and jingled along broad avenues; close to the Casino were its two great hotels, the Donjon and the Brittany, gay with awnings and piling sham Gothic turrets into the sky.

Eve stayed away from the Casino and the bars. After the headache and tension of life with Ned Atwood, she was both nerve-strung and bored: a dangerous combination. She was lonely, but she hated company. Sometimes she played golf — early in the morning, when there would be nobody else on the links — or rode horseback across the scrubby sand dunes by the sea.

And then she met Toby Lawes.

The Lawes family lived, rather disconcertingly, just opposite her in the rue des Anges. It was a short, narrow street, of white and pink stone houses in little walled gardens. But the street was so uncomfortably narrow that you could see clearly into the windows of the houses opposite. And this prompted disturbing reflections.

Several times during her life here with Ned, Eve had vaguely noticed the people across the street. There was an elderly man — he turned out to be Sir Maurice Lawes, Toby's father — who had once or twice looked very hard at them, as though perplexed. His kindly, ascetic face stuck in Eve's memory. There was a red-haired girl, and a cheerful elderly woman. But Eve had never seen Toby himself until that morning on the golf course.

It was a hot, still morning towards the middle of June. Few persons in La Bandelette were yet awake. The tees, the green fairways still gleaming with dew, the line of pine trees screening the sea, were held in a hollow of silence and heat. Eve, playing badly, landed in a sand trap at the approach to the third green.

Feeling mutinous and wretched after a sleepless night, she unslung the golf bag from her shoulder and flung it down. She felt she hated the game. She sat down on the edge of the sand trap, and stared at the position. She was still staring at it when a long brassy-shot screamed down the fairway, hooked, and thudded into the grass at the top of the bunker. The ball trickled over the edge of the bunker, and rolled down into the sand not three feet from her own.

"Idiot!" Eve said aloud.

It was followed, in a minute or two, by a young man who walked up the other side of the bunker and appeared over it against the skyline, looking down at her.

"Good God!" he said. "I didn't know you were there!"

"That's quite all right."

"I didn't mean to play through you! I should have yelled. I...."

He scrambled down the bunker into the sand, un-hitching a heavy bag containing about two dozen clubs. He was a strong, homely, rather starchy young man, with the pleasantest expression Eve had seen in a long time. His thick brown hair was cut close to his head. His small mustache gave him a vaguely man-of-the-world air which was contradicted by the lofty seriousness of his bearing.

He stood and stared at Eve. Everything about him was correct, except perhaps the rush of color to his face. You could see him desperately trying to prevent this, cursing up and down his soul, and, of course, getting redder than ever.

"I've seen you before," he declared.

"Really?" said Eve, conscious of not looking her best.

Then Toby Lawes's straightforwardness reached at one jump what might have taken his own brand of diplomacy months to achieve.

"Tell me," he said. "Are you still married or any-thing?"

They finished the round together. As early as the following afternoon, Toby Lawes was announcing that he had met a wonderful woman who had been married to a swine, but was bearing up in a way that must rouse the admiration of anybody.

Now, this was quite true. But such announcements are not, in general, very well received by the young man's family.

Eve, who thought she knew her world, imagined she could tell how this would affect the Lawes family. She could imagine the expressionless faces at the dinner table, the discreet cough or side-glance, the casual words, "Have you, Toby?" followed by a remark that it would be interesting to meet such a paragon. From the female members of the family, Lady Lawes and Toby's sister Janice, Eve expected a hostility hardly veiled by politeness.

She was therefore astounded at what happened.

They simply accepted her. She was invited to tea, in the luxuriant garden behind the Lawes's villa. Before either side had said ten words, both sides knew that it was all right and that it was going to be a friendship. These things happen. Even in the world as Ned Atwood knew it — and, unfortunately, as you and I often know it — such things happen..Eve's bewilderment changed to fervent gratitude; it thawed the ice of her nerves; it left her almost frightened because she was beginning to feel so happy.

Helena Lawes, Toby's mother, frankly liked Eve. The red-haired Janice, twenty-three years old, admired her beauty almost to the extent of a crush.

Uncle Ben, though he smoked his pipe and said little, invariably sided with her in an argument. Sir Maurice, the old man, often asked her opinion about some article in his collection. It was the accolade.

As for Toby . . .

Toby was a very good, very conscientious young man. This is not said as slander. If there was sometimes about him a vague suggestion of the stuffed shirt, his sense of humor redeemed it.

"After all, I've got to be," he pointed out.

"Got to be what?" asked red-haired Janice.

"Caesar's wife," said Toby. "As manager of the La Bandelette branch of Hookson's,"— even now the words gave him a pleasurable thrill,—"I've got to be cautious. London banks don't encourage racketting."

"But do any of them?" asked Janice. "I mean, even in French banks you seldom see the clerks hiding blondes under the counter or getting pie-eyed during business hours."

"I should think," Helena Lawes observed dreamily, "that a drunken bank would be one of the noblest things ever devised outside Thorne Smith."

Toby looked a little shocked. But he considered this seriously, smoothing at his small mustache.

"Hookson's," he said, "is one of the oldest banks in England. They've been at that place by Temple Bar ever since they were goldsmiths." He turned to

Eve. "In his collection Dad's got one of the little gold figures they used to use as an emblem."

This statement, as usual, was greeted by a tempered silence. Sir Maurice Lawes's hobby, his collection, hovered in status between a family joke and an appreciation on their part that among other junk he had got hold of some really beautiful things.

The collection was housed in his study, up on the first floor in a largish room overlooking the street. He usually sat up late over it. From her own bedroom window across the way, Eve and Ned Atwood had once or twice looked across in the bad old days, and seen the study with undrawn curtains: the old man holding a magnifying glass, the kindly face that stuck in her memory, and the glass-fronted cabinets along the walls.

No reference to those days was ever made now. So far as the Lawes family were concerned, Ned Atwood might never have existed. Sir Maurice Lawes, indeed, once began to touch on the subject in a veiled way; but he hesitated and drifted away from it, after a curious glance she could not understand.

And then, towards the end of July, Toby proposed marriage.

Eve never realized how much she had come to count on him; how much she cried out for stability, and laughter that was honest laughter. You could lean on Toby. If he sometimes treated her a little too much like a figure in a stained-glass window, this roused in her — paradoxically — a new tenderness.

In La Bandelette there used to be a modest restaurant, called the Restaurant of the Forest, where you dined in the open air under Chinese lanterns among the trees. Eve was looking particularly beautiful that night in pearl-gray which emphasized the warmth of her skin, pink-tinted rather than pale. Across the table from her sat Toby, twisting a knife in his fingers and looking anything but a stuffed shirt.

"Well?" he said directly. "I know I'm not worthy of you,"— how Ned Atwood would have guffawed at that! —"but I love you very much and I think I could make you happy."

"Hello, Eve," said a voice behind her shoulder.

For one horrible second she thought it was Ned who had spoken.

But, if it was not Ned, it was one of his friends. She had never expected to meet any of them at a place like the Restaurant of the Forest. As a rule, in the season, they dined at half-past ten and then went on to the Casino, where they sat all night at small, crafty betting. Eve recognized the face that was grinning at her, if she could not remember his name.

"Dance?" invited Mr. Nameless, in his bored voice.

"Thanks, no. I'm not dancing tonight."

"Oh. Sorry," murmured Mr. Nameless, and drifted away. His eyes reminded her of a certain party; it seemed to her that he almost laughed in her face.

"Friend of yours?" asked Toby.

"No," answered Eve. The orchestra was playing again, a waltz of a few years back. "A friend of my ex-husband."

Toby kept clearing his throat. His may have been merely a romantic fondness, an idealized conception of a woman that never existed, but it hurt him like physical pain. They had never discussed Ned Atwood: that is, Eve had never told Toby the truth about Ned. The differences, she had said, were temperamental. "He's rather nice, really." And this light comment had got into Toby Lawes's stolid soul with the strongest barb of jealousy.

For the dozenth time he cleared his throat.

"About this other matter," he said. "I mean, asking you to marry me. If you'd like time to think it over . . ."

The music of the orchestra, flowing over Eve's mind, brought back sordid memory.

"I — I know I'm not all I should be," pursued Toby, fidgeting and putting down the knife. "But if you could give me a sort of business man's idea of whether the answer might be yes or no . . ."

Eve put her hands across the table.

"Yes," she said. "Yes, yes, yes!"

For fully ten seconds Toby did not say anything. He moistened his lips. He put his hands over hers, but delicately, as though still touching stained glass; and then, with a belated remembrance of making a show of himself in public, quickly withdrew them. The reverence of his look surprised Eve and rather disturbed her. It occurred to her to wonder whether Toby Lawes knew *anything* about women.

"Well?" she asked.

Toby considered this.

"I think we'd better have another drink," he decided. Then he shook his head, in a slow and startled way. "You know, this is the happiest day of my life."

On the last day of July, their engagement was announced.

A fortnight later, Ned Atwood, in the bar of the Plaza in New York, heard about it from an acquaintance who had just arrived. For some minutes he sat perfectly still, twisting the stem of his glass round and round. Then he went out and booked passage to sail by the *Normandie* two days afterwards.

And so, all unsuspected by any of these three, black tragedy was gathering round a certain villa in the rue des Anges.

II

IT WAS a quarter to one in the morning when Ned Atwood turned off the Boulevard du Casino into the rue des Anges.

Distantly, the beam of the great lighthouse swept the sky. The intense heat of that day had begun to cool, but waves of it still seemed to rise from baked asphalt. Hardly a footstep sounded in La Bandelette. The few visitors who still remained at the dead-end of the season were at the Casino, playing until dawn.

Therefore nobody saw the youngish-looking man in the fuzzy dark suit and soft hat, who hesitated at the mouth of the rue des Anges before diving into it. He kept his teeth clenched, and his eyes were as glassy as though he had been drinking. But on this night at least Ned had not been drinking, except of a certain emotion.

Eve had never ceased to love him: this was the fact of which he had convinced himself.

It had been unwise — he would have admitted it now — to boast that afternoon in the bar of the Donjon Hotel that he was going to win her back. That had been the error. He should have slipped quietly back to La Bandelette, as quietly as he was now slipping along the rue des Anges, with a key to Eve's villa in his hand.

The Villa Miramar, where she lived, was halfway down on the left hand side. As he approached, Ned instinctively glanced across the street at the house opposite. Like Eve's villa, that of the Lawes family was large and square, of white stone with a bright red tiled roof. Like Eve's, it was set back a few feet from the street behind a high wall and a little iron-grilled gate.

And Ned saw what he expected to see. Ground floor, dark. Floor above, dark except for the two glowing windows of Sir Maurice Lawes's study. The steel shutters were folded back from these windows; the curtains had not been drawn against that hot night.

"All right!" Ned said aloud, and drew the sweet-scented air into his lungs.

Though he could hardly be afraid that the old man would hear him, and no reason to give a curse anyway, still he walked softly. He opened the gate in the wall round Eve's villa. He hurried up the short path to the front door. His key to the front door, retained from happier or at least more turbulent days, he fitted into the lock; again he breathed deeply, said a prayer to the pagan gods in his mind, and shouldered forward according to plan.

Was Eve awake or asleep? The absence of lights at the Villa Miramar meant nothing. It had always been Eve's habit — a morbidly respectable one, he had called it — to keep every window sealed up with curtains after nightfall.

But the downstairs hall was dark. It had that smell of furniture polish and coffee which seems to haunt French houses: it brought back every detail of the past. He groped across to the staircase, and tiptoed up.

It was a narrow, graceful staircase with a balustrade of filigree bronze, fitted against the wall like the curve of a shell. But it was also tall and steep, and its thick carpet was fastened by old-fashioned brass stair rods. How many times he had gone up those stairs in the dark! How many times he had heard the clock tick, and felt the devil stir in his heart; because he loved her and (he thought) she probably wasn't faithful to him. One of the stair rods, he remembered — near the top, not far from Eve's bedroom door — was loose. He had tripped on it many times, and once he swore it would be the death of him.

Ned guided himself with one hand on the banister rail. Eve was still awake. He could see a thin line of light under the door of her bedroom at the front. In his preoccupation with that light, he forgot all about the loose stair rod he had sworn to avoid; and, of course, he fell flat over it.

"Hell!" he said aloud.

In her bedroom, Eve Neill heard that noise.

She knew who it was.

Eve was sitting before the mirror of the dressing-table, brushing her hair with slow, steady sweeps of the brush. A hanging lamp above the mirror, the only light in that room, brought out the warmth of her coloring: the fleece of light chestnut hair, falling to her shoulders, and the luminousness of the gray eyes. When her head was pulled backwards to the sweep of the brush, it showed the roundness of her neck above the defiant set of the shoulders. She was wearing white silk pajamas and white satin mules.

Eve did not turn round. She continued to brush her hair. But she felt a second's blind panic before — behind her back — the door opened, and she saw Ned Atwood's face reflected in the mirror.

Ned, though cold sober, was almost crying.

"Look here," he began, before the door had fully opened, "you can't *do* it!"

Eve heard herself speaking. Her panic had not lessened: it was increasing. But she continued to brush her hair, perhaps to hide the twitching of a nerve in her arm.

"I thought it was you," she said quietly. "Have you gone completely out of your mind?"

"No! I —"

"Sh-h, for heaven's sake!"

"I love you," said Ned, and spread out his hands.

"You swore to me you'd lost that key. So you lied to me again?"

"This is no time for arguing trivialities," said Ned, who clearly felt it as the worst of trivialities. "Are you really going to marry this fellow," he spat out the word, "Lawes?"

"Yes."

Both of them instinctively glanced towards the two closely curtained windows overlooking the street. Both of them, it appeared, had the same thought.

"Can I interest you," asked Eve, "in elementary decency?"

"Not as long as I love you."

No doubt about it: he was almost crying. A piece of acting? Eve doubted it. Something, for the moment at least, had cracked across the languid mockery and magnificent self-assurance with which he faced the world. But this quickly passed. Ned became himself again. He strolled across, threw his hat on the bed, and sat down in an easy chair.

With difficulty, Eve kept herself from screaming.

"Across the street . . ." she began.

"I know, I know!"

"You know what?" asked Eve. She put down the brush and swung round on the dressing-table stool to face him.

"The old man, Sir Maurice Lawes . . ."

"Oh? And what do you happen to know about *him*?"

"He sits up every night," answered Ned, "in a room across the street. Over his collection, or whatever it is. From those windows you can see straight into this room here."

It was very warm in the bedroom, which smelled of bath-salts and cigarettes. At ease in the chair, one long leg hooked over the arm of it, Ned surveyed the room. His face sharpened with mockery. It was not only a ruggedly good-looking face: in the forehead, the eyes, the lines round the mouth, it was an imaginative and even intellectual face.

He looked round the familiar walls, panelled in dark red satin. He looked at the many mirrors. He looked at the bed, where his hat now lay on the coverlet. He looked at the telephone by the bed. He looked at the solitary light over the dressing-table.

"They're very holy, aren't they?" he suggested.

"Who?"

"The Lawes family. If the old man knew you

were entertaining an obviously welcome guest at one o'clock in the morning . . ."

Eve started to get up, but sat down again.

"Don't worry," Ned added harshly. "I'm not quite such a swine as you think I am."

"Then will you *please* get out of here?"

His tone grew desperate.

"All I want to know," he insisted, "is *why*? Why are you marrying this bloke?"

"Because I happen to be in love with him."

"Rubbish," said Ned with calm arrogance, and brushed this aside.

"How long," said Eve, "will it take you to finish what you've got to say?"

"It can't be money," he was musing. "You've got more of that than you can possibly need. No, my sugar-candy witch: it's not money. On the contrary."

"What do you mean: on the contrary?"

Ned used a horrible directness.

"Why do you think the old goat over there is so anxious to marry his stuffed-shirt son to you? It's your money, my darling. And, so help me, that's all it is."

Eve could have picked up the brush and flung it at him. He was breaking down, as he usually did, everything she had tried to build up. He was sitting back at ease, his necktie fallen out over the coat of his rough dark suit, and the troubled air of one who honestly tries to solve a problem. Eve's chest hurt her, and she wanted to cry herself.

"And I suppose," she blazed at him, "*you* know so much about the Lawes family?"

He took this seriously.

"I don't know them, no. But I've picked up all the information I could about them. And the key to the whole business . . ."

"While we're on the subject," said Eve, "suppose you give me back that key of yours."

"Key?"

"The key to this house. The key you're twirling round your finger on the key-ring now. I should like to make certain this is the last time you put me in such an embarrassing position."

"Eve, for God's sake!"

"Lower your voice, please."

"You're coming back to me," said Ned, sitting up straight. Then his voice grew querulous as he saw the expression on her face. "What's wrong with you? You've changed."

"Have I?"

"Why this excess of holiness all of a sudden? You used to be a human being. Now you're all hoity-toity and God knows what. Since you met this Lawes family, your virtue would make Lucrece ashamed of her-self."

"Really?"

Ned jumped to his feet during a dangerous and hard-breathing silence.

"And don't sit there saying, 'really,' and putting your nose in the air. You can't tell me you're in love with this Toby Lawes. I dare you to tell me that!"

"Just what have you got against Toby Lawes, Ned dear?"

"Nothing, except that everybody says he's a moron and a stuffed shirt. He may be all right: he may be the grand high muck-a-muck. But he's not your sort. For better or worse, I am."

Eve shuddered.

"Now what the devil," shouted Ned, addressing a mirror, "can you do with a woman like this?" Then he paused. "I suppose," he added, with an expression she knew only too well from the past, "there's only one thing I ought to do."

Eve also jumped up.

"Your sex-appeal," said Ned, "especially in those pajamas, would make an anchorite forget himself. And I'm no anchorite."

"Don't you dare come near me!"

"I feel," said Ned, with sudden despondency, "like a villain in a melodrama. With the heroine cringing in front of me, afraid to call out in case . . ." He nodded towards the window. Then his expression changed. "All right," he said slyly. "Why not be a villain? Why not be a creeping blackguard? *You'll* enjoy it."

"I'll scratch! I warn you!"

"Good for you. That's more like it."

"Ned, I'm not joking!"

"Neither am I. You'll scratch. But only at first. I don't mind that."

"You've always sworn you had no sense of decency. But you used to pride yourself on a sense of fair play. If —"

"You don't think the old goat across the road can hear anything do you?"

"Ned, what are you doing? *Come back from that window!*"

Belatedly, Eve remembered the light over the dressing-table. She groped above her head and switched it off, plunging the room into darkness. The windows were shrouded with heavy damask curtains; there were lace curtains underneath, veiling the open casement. A breath of cooler air stirred as Ned, fumbling among damask folds, drew back a corner of them. He meant to cause no real embarrassment to Eve unless it became absolutely necessary; and what he saw reassured him.

"Is Maurice Lawes still up? Is he?"

"Yes, he's still up. But he's not paying any attention. He's got a magnifying glass, and he's looking at some kind of snuff-box thing. — Hold on!"

"What is it?"

"There's somebody with him; but I can't see who it is."

"Toby, probably." Eve's whisper rose to a kind of stifled shriek. "Ned Atwood, *will* you come away from that window?"

This was the point at which they both became conscious that the light was out.

A faint whitish glow filtered in from the rue des Anges, illuminating the side of Ned's face as he turned round. His naïveté of manner, his childlike surprise at finding the room in darkness, were betrayed by the mocking expression of his mouth. He dropped the lace netting and drew the curtains, shutting down a lid of darkness.

The room seemed overpoweringly hot. Again Eve groped over her head for the switch of the hanging lamp — and failed to find it. Instead of groping still further, she backed away from the dressing-table stool and blundered across the room away from him.

"Eve, listen . . ."

"This is getting rather ridiculous. Will you turn on the light, please?"

"How can I turn on the light? You're closer to it!"

"No, I'm not. I'm . . ."

"Oh," said Ned in a curious voice.

She caught that inflection, and it frightened her still more. It was a note of triumph.

What he would not understand, or in his simple vanity could not understand, was that she found him repulsive. The situation was more than merely awkward: it had become a nightmare. And, of all possible ways out, the one solution which would never have occurred to her was to call for help — call the servants for instance — and end this.

Eve Neill, quite simply, had got used to the idea that nobody ever believed *her* version of any incident like this. Nobody ever had, and nobody ever would. This was her experience of life. To tell the truth, she was almost as much afraid of the servants' knowing as of having it known to the Lawes family. Servants gossiped. Whispered behind each successive hand, their stories grew more decorated at every telling. The new maid Yvette, for instance . . .

"Give me one good reason," Ned was saying coolly, "why you're marrying this fellow Lawes."

Her voice came piercing out of the dark, even though it was not loud.

"For God's sake go away. You don't believe I'm in love with him. But it's true. Anyway, I haven't got to explain my actions to you. Not any longer. Do you think you have any claim on me?"

"Yes."

"What claim?"

"I'm coming over there to show you."

In the dark, as clearly as though he could see her, he knew what she was doing. By the rustling sound, the creak of a spring, he could tell that she had caught up the heavy lace negligée that lay across the foot of the bed, and was starting to put it on. She had struggled into it, all except one sleeve, by the time he reached her.

There was another fear, too. Eve had not failed to think of it. No woman — so her more worldly acquaintances had always assured her — ever forgets the first man in her physical life. She may think it forgotten, yet it remains. Eve was a human being; she had been alone for many months; and Ned Atwood, whatever else you might say, had a way with him. What if . . . ?

She struck out at him, fiercely but clumsily, as he caught her.

"Let go! You're hurting me!"

"Are you going to be good?"

"No! Ned, the servants . . . !"

"Nonsense. There's only old Mopsy."

"Mopsy's gone. There's a new maid. And I don't

trust her. I think she spies. Anyway, can't you *please* have the ordinary decency to . . ."

"Are you going to be good?"

"No!"

Eve was tall, only two inches below his own height. But she was slender and soft of body, without any great physical strength. By this time it must have been apparent, even to Ned's befuddled wits, that there was something wrong: that this was not co-quetry, but real resistance. Such things are atmos-pheres, and Ned Atwood was no fool. But, with his arms round Eve, he had now completely lost his head.

And it was at this point, shatteringly, that the tele-phone rang.

III

THE blatancy of a ringing telephone is anywhere bad. Here, piercing the dark of the bedroom, it had a clamour and clatter of accusation. It would not shut up. Both of them, startled out of their wits, spoke in low voices as though the telephone could overhear.

"Don't answer it, Eve!"

"Let me go! Suppose it's . . . ?"

"Nonsense! Let it ring!"

"But suppose they've seen . . . ?"

They were standing within reach of the telephone-table. Eve had instinctively stretched out her hand to take it; and he seized her wrist to prevent her. As a result, with a scuffle and clink the phone bumped off its cradle-hook as the base slid too, and fell with a rattling thump on the table. The shrilling peals were cut off. But in the silence they could both clearly hear a tiny voice — Toby Lawes's voice.

"Hello? Eve?" it said in the dark.

Ned dropped her arms and backed away. He had never heard the voice before; but it was not difficult to guess to whom it belonged.

"Hello? Eve?"

Eve groped after the sliding phone, and banged it against the wall before she could finally pick it up. Her hard breathing slowed down. Any disinterested person must have admired her. When she spoke, she sounded controlled and almost casual.

"Yes? Is that you, Toby?"

Toby Lawes had a heavy, slow-speaking voice. Reduced to that microcosm by the telephone, its every syllable was audible to both listeners.

"Sorry to wake you up in the middle of the night," Toby said. "But I couldn't sleep. I had to ring you. Do you mind?"

Ned Atwood blundered across and switched on the light over the dressing-table.

It might have been thought that Eve would glare at him for this. She did nothing of the kind. Aside from a quick glance to make sure the curtains were drawn, she hardly seemed to notice it: or even notice him. To judge by Toby's apologetic cheerfulness, Eve had nothing to fear. But that was not all. Toby spoke with such concentrated tenderness that to the self-centered Ned — who could not imagine any man except himself speaking like this — it sounded startling and rather grotesque.

Ned started to grin. But something else very quickly wiped the amusement off his face.

"Toby darling!" Eve breathed.

There could be no mistaking it. It was the tone of a woman who is in love, or thinks she is. Her face was radiant. Her relief, her gratitude, seemed to pour out to him.

"You didn't mind my ringing up?" Toby demanded.

"Toby, of course not! How — how are you?"

"I'm fine. Only I couldn't sleep."

"I mean, where are you?"

"I'm downstairs in the drawing-room," replied the engrossed Mr. Lawes, who clearly saw nothing odd in this query. "I was up in my room. But I kept on thinking about how lovely you are, so I had to ring you up."

"Toby, darling!"

("Rats!" said Ned Atwood).

There is always something particularly inane about the spectacle of somebody else's emotion, even though you may happen to share the sentiments yourself.

"I mean it," Toby assured her seriously. "Er — did you like the play we saw the English Players do tonight?"

("Does he ring up to discuss dramatic criticism at this time in the morning?" asked Ned. "Shut the blighter off!")

"Toby, I did so enjoy it! I think Shaw is rather sweet."

("Shaw," said Ned. "Sweet. Oh, my God!")

Yet, as he watched the expression on Eve's face, he had reason for feeling rather sick.

Toby sounded troubled.

"I thought parts of the play were rather broad, though. You weren't shocked, were you?"

("I don't believe it," muttered Ned, opening his eyes wide and staring at the telephone. "I just don't believe it!")

"Mother and Janice and Uncle Ben," pursued Toby, "said it was all right. But I don't know." Toby was one of those people whom the views of Mr. Shaw rouse to a state of exasperated bewilderment. "I may be a bit old-fashioned. All the same, it does seem to me that there are certain things that no women, no well-bred women I mean, need to know anything about."

"I wasn't shocked, Toby dear."

"Well," temporized Mr. Lawes. You could imagine him fidgeting at the other end of the phone. "That's — that's all I wanted to say, really."

("Quite a Cavalier poet, by George!")

But Toby gulped at something else. "Remember, we're going picnicking tomorrow. It ought to be glorious weather. Oh, and by the way. The old man got a new trinket for his collection tonight. He's as pleased as Punch."

("Yes," sneered Ned. "We saw the old goat gloating over it a minute ago.")

"Yes, Toby," agreed Eve. "We saw —"

She blurted this out, and it was as near a slip as makes no difference. Again sheer blind panic swam across her wits. She glanced up, seeing on Ned's face the crooked smile which could be so detestable or so charming. But her voice flowed on:

"I mean, we saw an *awfully* nice play tonight."

"It was, wasn't it?" said Toby. "But I mustn't keep you out of bed any longer. Good night, dear."

"Good night, Toby. You don't know, you'll never be able to guess, how glad I've been to hear from you!"

She replaced the phone, and then there was silence.

Eve still sat on the edge of the bed, one hand on the telephone and the other holding her lace negligée to her breast. She raised her head and looked at Ned. There was color in her cheeks, under the gray eyes. Her long silky hair, framing the delicacy of the face, gleamed rich and brown and rather dishevelled. She lifted a hand to smooth it back. The pink fingernails shone, and contrasted with the whiteness of the arm. In that sense of remoteness while being so near, of potential passion arrested while still kindling through the blood, she was lovely enough to turn any man's brain.

Ned watched her. Taking cigarettes and a lighter from his pocket, he lit a cigarette and inhaled deeply. The flame of the lighter wabbled in his hand before he snapped it out. All his nerves were twitching, though he tried not to show it. The hot, heavy silence of the room was unbroken even by the ticking of a clock.

And Ned was in no hurry.

"All right," he ventured at length. He had to clear his throat. "Say it."

"Say what?"

" 'Take your hat and go.' "

"Take your hat," repeated Eve calmly, "and go."

"I see." He examined the tip of the cigarette, inhaled smoke again, and blew it out. "Conscience bothering you, is it?"

This was not true. But there was just enough of a fleeting grain of truth in it to make Eve's face flame. Ned, tall and lounging, still seemed to be studying the end of the cigarette while he pursued this with devilish detective instincts.

"Tell me, my sugar-candy witch. Don't you ever have any qualms?"

"About what?"

"Life with the Lawes family."

"You see, Ned, you simply wouldn't understand."

"I'm not 'fine' enough, eh? Like that moron across the street?"

Eve got to her feet, and adjusted her negligée. It was tied round the waist with a band of pink satin which was always coming untied, and she knotted it again.

"You would be more impressive," she said, "if you didn't talk so much like a sulky child."

"Yes, and that's another thing. When you talk to him, your style of conversation depresses me beyond endurance."

"Really?"

"Yes, really. You're an intelligent woman."

"Thank you."

"But, when you talk to Toby Lawes, you seem determined to gear your mentality to his. Cripes, how you gush! Shaw is 'sweet.' You'll end by passionately convincing yourself that you're as stupid as he is. Or will you? If you have to talk to the fellow like that before you're married, what will it be like afterwards?" He spoke softly. "Don't you *ever* have any qualms, Eve?"

(Damn you!)

"What's the matter?" inquired Ned, blowing up another cloud of smoke. "Don't you dare listen to the devil's advocate?"

"I'm not afraid of you."

"What do you know about this Lawes family, really?"

"What did I know about you, before we were married? What have I ever learned since about your life before you met me, if it comes to that? Except that you're selfish ..."

"Agreed."

"Beastly ... !"

"Eve dear, we were talking about the Lawes family. What have you fallen for? Their respectability?"

"Of course I want to be respectable. Every woman does."

"Yah!"

"That's unworthy of your cleverness, darling. You see, I like them. I like Mama Lawes and Papa Lawes and Toby and Janice and Uncle Ben. They're friendly people. They do the right thing, and yet they're not stodgy. They're so," — she searched her mind, —"so *sane*."

"And Papa Lawes likes your bank-account."

"Don't you *dare* say that!"

"I can't prove it. But one day ..."

Ned paused. He drew the back of his hand across his forehead. For a moment he stood looking at her with what she could have sworn was real affection: a new thing, a perplexed and desperate thing, even a kindly thing.

"Eve," he said abruptly, "I'm not going to let you do it."

"Do what?"

"I'm not going to let you make a mistake."

As he walked over to crush out his cigarette in the glass tray of the dressing-table, Eve's body went rigid. She stared at him. Knowing him as she did, she sensed a certain mood. Ned turned round again. There were fine little horizontal wrinkles across his shiny forehead, under the crisp fair hair.

"Eve, I learned something at the Donjon today."

"Well?"

"Papa Lawes, they say," he went on, blowing out smoke and nodding towards the windows, "is rather deaf. Still, if I whopped back the curtains and shouted out to ask how he's getting on . . ."

Silence.

A feeling of physical illness, grotesquely like the beginning of seasickness, began in Eve's stomach and seemed to spread so that it blurred even her eyesight. Nothing seemed quite real. The cigarette-smoke was choking in that hot room. She saw Ned's blue eyes looking at her out of smoke. She heard her own voice speaking with small and far-away effect.

"You couldn't play a filthy trick like that!"

"Couldn't I?"

"No! Not even you!"

"But is it a filthy trick?" Ned asked quietly. He pointed his finger at her. "What have you done? You're perfectly innocent, aren't you?"

"Yes!"

"I tell you again: you've been a model of virtue. I'm the villain of the piece. I forced my way in here, even if I did have a key." He held it up. "Suppose I did kick up a row? What have *you* got to be afraid of?"

Her lips felt dry. Everything seemed to take place in a void, where lights splintered and sounds took a long time to reach you.

"I'm a bounder who ought to be thrashed — that is, if Toby Lawes can do it. You tried to throw me out, didn't you? And, of course, your loyal friends know you and they'll believe that as soon as you tell them? All right! *I* won't deny your story, I promise you. If you really loathe and despise me, if these people are all you say they are, why don't you shout out yourself instead of having a fit when I threaten to do it?"

"Ned, I can't explain it . . ."

"Why not?"

"Because you wouldn't understand!"

"Why not?"

Eve threw out her arms in a helplessness beyond speech. Explain the world, in half a dozen words?

"I can only tell you this," Eve said. She spoke quietly, though her eyes brimmed over. "I'd rather die than have anybody know you were here tonight."

Ned stood looking at her for a moment.

"Would you, by God?" he said. And he turned round and walked rapidly towards the windows.

Eve's first instinct was to turn the light out. She ran forwards, almost tripping in the heavy folds of her negligée, whose satin waistband had come untied again. Afterwards she could never remember whether or not she had screamed at him. Stumbling over the dressing-table stool, she reached up for the switch of the hanging lamp, found it, swayed on her feet, and could have cried out with relief when the room went dark.

Now it may be accounted as doubtful whether Ned — even in his present state of mind — had ever really meant to shout across the street at Sir Maurice Lawes. But, in any case, it would have made no difference.

He flung back the brocade curtains, rattling on their wooden rings. He lifted the net curtains underneath, and peered out. But that was all he did.

He was looking straight across the street — not fifty feet away — into the lighted windows of Sir Maurice Lawes's study. They were full-length windows, after the French fashion. They opened out on a little stone and wrought-iron balcony just above the front door. These windows stood partly open; their steel shutters were not closed; the curtains gaped open.

But the study inside did not look as it had looked when Ned first glanced across there, only a few minutes ago.

"Ned!" said Eve in a voice of rising terror.

No reply.

"Ned! *What is it?*"

He pointed, and that was enough.

They saw a medium-sized square room, its walls lined with glass-fronted curio-cabinets of odd styles and shapes. Those two windows allowed a view of nearly all the room. A bookcase or two interrupted the line of the curio-cabinets. The furniture was spindly gilt and brocade, against white walls and a gray blur of a carpet. When Ned had last looked across there, only the desk lamp had been burning. Now the blaze of the central chandelier picked out that sight with a more horrible clarity than either of the two watchers could endure.

Through the left-hand window, they could see Sir Maurice Lawes's big flat-topped table-desk against the left-hand wall. Through the right-hand window, they could see the white marble fireplace in the right-hand wall. And at the back of the study —

that is, in the back wall facing them — they could see the door leading to the upstairs hall.

Someone, as they watched, was softly closing that door.

They saw it move as a certain person slipped out of the study. Eve arrived just too late to catch a glimpse of a face which was to haunt her afterwards. But Ned saw it.

Hidden by the closing door, somebody stretched out a hand — it seemed a small hand, at that distance — in a brownish-colored glove. This hand touched the light switch at one side of the door. A curled and capable finger pressed the switch down, extinguishing the central lights. Then the tall white door, with its metal handle instead of a knob, was gently closed.

Now only the desk lamp, a small office lamp with a green glass shade, shed a dim light down on the big flat-topped table-desk pushed against the left-hand wall, and on the swivel-chair drawn up to it. Sir Maurice Lawes, whom they could see in profile, sat in his usual swivel-chair. But he was not now holding a magnifying glass; and he would never hold a magnifying glass again.

The magnifying glass lay on the desk blotter. Over that blotter — over the whole surface of the table — were scattered fragments of something that had been smashed there. Many fragments. Curious fragments.

Transparent fragments which shone pinkly, and gleamed and reflected back the light, as though through rose-tinted snow. Gold seemed to be among those fragments. Perhaps something else as well. But colors were difficult to discern because of all the blood-splashes, across the desk and even up the wall.

How long Eve Neill stood there, hypnotized, with nausea rising in her throat yet refusing to credit what she saw, she could never afterwards remember.

"Ned, I'm going to be . . ."

"*Quiet!*"

Sir Maurice Lawes's head had been beaten in by repeated blows from some weapon not now visible. His knees, wedged against the opening of the table-desk, had prevented his body from sliding down out of the chair. His chin was on his breast; his limp hands hung down. Blood, descending like a painted mask across his face and along the cheek to a point below the nose, made a kind of cap for that motionless head.

IV

In such fashion died Maurice Lawes, knight, formerly of Queen Anne's Gate, Westminster, and late of the rue des Anges, La Bandelette.

In those far-off days when newspapers had little to print and much paper to print it on, his death created a stir in the English press. True, few people even knew who he was, let alone why he had got his knighthood, until somebody mysteriously murdered him. Then everything about him became of interest. A knighthood, they discovered, had been the reward for his humanitarian activities in the old days. He had been interested in slum clearance, interested in prison reform, interested in seamen's betterment.

Who's Who listed his hobbies as "collecting and human nature." He was one of those contradictory characters who, a few years later, were to bring England almost to ruin. Though he gave large sums to charity, and was always badgering the authorities about spending for betterment, he himself lived abroad to avoid the iniquity of paying income tax. Short, tubby, rather deaf, with a mustache and little tuft of chin beard, he also lived in a world of his own.

45

But his qualities as a popular man, a kindly man, a pleasant man in his own household, received their full tribute. And it was a deserved tribute. Maurice Lawes really was just what he pretended to be.

So, with studied and ferocious brutality, somebody smashed in his head. And, at the window overlooking a quiet street, at that drugged hour of the morning, Eve Neill and Ned Atwood stood like a pair of frightened children.

What Eve could not endure was the sight of the lamplight shining on the blood. She dodged back beside the window, and would not look any longer.

"Ned, come away from there!"

Her companion made no reply.

"Ned, he's not really . . . ?"

"Yes. At least, I think so. You can't tell from here."

"Maybe he's only hurt."

Again her companion made no reply. Of these two, you would have said that the man was more astounded than the woman. But this was only natural. For he had seen something which she had not seen. He had seen the face of Brown-Gloves. He continued to peer across at the lighted room, his heart thumping and his throat as dry as sand.

"*I said, maybe he's only hurt!*"

Ned cleared his throat. "You mean you think we'd better . . . ?

"We couldn't go over there," whispered Eve, as the full terror of the situation came to her, "even if we wanted to."

"No. I — I suppose not."

"What happened to him?"

Ned started to speak, but checked himself. This situation was too good (or too bad) to be true. Words would not do. Instead he made the pantomime of one who swings up some weapon and strikes down, savagely. Both their voices were hoarse. When they spoke above a whisper, the words seemed to ring out and echo up among the chimney-pots, and they instantly fell silent again. Once more Ned cleared his throat.

"Have you got anything to look through? Field-glasses? Opera-glasses?"

"Why?"

"Never mind. Have you got them?"

Field-glasses. Standing rigidly with her back to the wall beside the window, Eve tried to fix her thoughts on this. Field-glasses, racing. Racing, Longchamps. She had been at Longchamps with the Lawes family only a few weeks ago. Memory returned in flashes of color and thuds of sound: the belling, colored shirts of the jockeys, and the pouring of horses past a white rail, while a bright sun shone. Maurice Lawes had worn a gray top-hat, and kept a pair of binoculars at his eyes. Uncle Ben, as usual, had betted and lost.

Stumbling, not guessing or even caring why Ned wanted the glasses, Eve moved across in the dark to a tallboy. From the top drawer she took out a pair of binoculars in their leather case, and thrust them into his hands.

The room opposite was much darker now that the central lights had been extinguished. But, when he trained the glasses on the right-hand window, adjusting their little wheel for focus, a segment of that room sharpened and sprang out at him.

He could see diagonally across to the right-hand wall and the mantelpiece. The mantelpiece was of white marble, and above it on the wall hung a bronze medallion head of the Emperor Napoleon. The fireplace was empty in this August weather, shielded by a small tapestry fire screen. But beside the grate was a stand of brass-headed fire irons: shovel, tongs, and poker.

"If that poker," he began, "has been . . ."

"Been what?"

"Have a look through these."

"I can't!"

For one horrible second she thought he was going to laugh in her face. But even Ned Atwood was not ironist enough for this. His face showed white like damp paper, and his hands shook when he tried to thrust the binoculars back into their case.

"Such a sane household," he observed, nodding towards where a bloody dead man sat sunk forward among his curios. "Such a sane household, I think you said."

The lump in Eve's throat felt as though it would choke her. "Are you telling me you *saw* who it was?"

"Yes. I am telling you just that."

"The burglar hit him, and you saw it?"

"I didn't see the dirty work actually done, no. Brown-gloves had finished by the time I looked out."

"What *did* you see?"

"Brown-gloves hanging up the poker in the stand, after the business was finished."

"Could you identify the burglar, if you saw him again?"

"I wish you'd stop using that word."

"What word?"

"Burglar."

In the lighted study across the street, once more the door opened.

But this time there was no furtiveness about it. The door moved and swung briskly, as though with determination. In the aperture appeared no more formidable a figure than that of Helena Lawes.

Despite bad lighting, Helena's every movement and gesture was always so eloquent that it was as though she stood within touching distance. You seemed to read every thought in her mind. As she opened the door, her lips moved. Whether by deduction or lip-reading or a combination of both, the watchers almost imagined they could hear the words she spoke.

"Maurice, you really *must* come to bed!"

Helena — whom nobody ever called Lady Lawes — was a middle-sized stoutish woman with a jovial round face and silver-gray bobbed hair. She cradled round her a brilliant Oriental kimono, hands buried in the sleeves, and her slippers flapped uncompromisingly. She stopped at the door, and spoke again. She switched on the central lights. Then she cradled her arms tighter, padding forward to speak to her husband, whose back was turned towards her.

Being short-sighted, Helena did not stop until she had almost reached him. Her shadow was thrown out into the street, wavering, as she passed the first window. She disappeared, and was seen again at the second.

In the thirty years of her married life, Helena Lawes had seldom been seen upset. It was therefore all the more unnerving when she backed away and began to scream — shrill screams which did not stop, which tore the night-quiet, which went shaking and piercing out into the street as though they would rouse each individual room in each individual house.

Eve Neill spoke quietly.

"Ned, you've got to go. Hurry!"

Still her companion did not move.

Eve seized his arm. "Helena will come after *me*! She always does. And then there's the police. They'll be swarming all over here in half a minute. If you don't go now, we're done for!" Her voice had become a moan of terror, and she kept shaking at his arm. "Ned, you didn't really mean what you said? About wanting to shout and give us away?"

He put up his hands and pressed the long, strong-knuckled fingers over his eyes. His shoulders bent forward.

"No. I didn't mean it. I was half out of my mind, that's all. I'm sorry."

"Then will you please go?"

"Yes. Eve, I swear I never meant —!"

"Your hat's on the bed. Here." She flew towards it, groping and patting at the eiderdown. "You'll have to find your own way down in the dark. I daren't turn on a light now."

"Why not?"

"Yvette! My new maid!"

A picture of Yvette, elderly, capable, slow-moving yet deft, rose in her mind. Though Yvette never spoke an unnecessary word, her every movement seemed a comment of some kind. Even for Toby Lawes she had a peculiar attitude which Eve could not understand. To Eve, Yvette symbolized the world which talked and talked and talked and talked. Suddenly she thought what might happen if she were forced to go into the witness-box in open court and say:

"At the time Sir Maurice Lawes was murdered, there was a man in my room. But, of course, it was perfectly innocent."

Of course, of course, of course: a giggle, and then laughter breaking like rockets. Aloud she said:

"Yvette sleeps on the floor above. She's sure to wake up. Those screams are going to wake up the whole street."

The screaming, in fact, was still going on. Eve wondered how long she could bear it. She found the hat and flung it at Ned.

"Tell me, Eve. Have you honestly and truly fallen for that holy blighter?"

"What holy blighter?"

"Toby Lawes."

"Oh, is this the *time* to talk about that?"

"Any time before you're dead," returned Ned, "is the time to talk about a love affair."

Even then she could not resist a spiteful dig.

"You've taught that to so many women, haven't you?"

"Yes. But to only one that ever mattered. And, what's more, you know it."

Still he didn't budge. Eve could have screamed herself. She kept opening and shutting her hands in spasmodic gestures, as though her will-power could force him towards the door like a series of physical pushes.

Across the road, Helena's outbursts had stopped. It left a void against the ear-drums: you waited for the noise of hurrying footsteps which would mean an *agent de police*. And a quick glance out of the window showed Eve something else.

Helena Lawes had now been joined by two other persons, her very pretty daughter Janice, and her brother Ben. They came blundering in at the door as though blinded by the lights. Eve could see Janice's red hair and the heavy, harassed face of Uncle Ben. In the night stillness fragments of disjointed words, half-heard, floated across the street as voices rose.

Ned's voice roused her.

"Steady!" he urged. "In another second you'll be having hysterics yourself. Just keep your shirt on and don't worry. They won't see me. I'll slip out the back way."

"Before you go, give me back that key."

He raised innocent eyebrows, but she flew at him.
"Don't pretend to misunderstand! You're *not* going to keep that front-door key any longer! Please!"

"No, darling. The key stays with me."

"You say you're sorry, don't you? Then if you've got any decency at all, after the position you've put me in tonight . . ." She felt rather than saw him hesitate, in the contrition he always showed when he had got somebody into trouble. "And, if you do, maybe I'll — see you again."

"You mean that?"

"Give me the key!"

A second later she almost wished she hadn't asked for it. It seemed to take an incredible, creeping, dragging time for him to detach the key from the ring. She hadn't meant what she had said about seeing him again; but she had reached so confused a state that she would have promised anything. She dropped the key for safe-keeping into the breast-pocket of her pajamas, and impelled him towards the door.

The upstairs hall was quiet and nearly dark. Yvette, on the floor above, had evidently not been roused. A dim shimmer fell into it from an uncurtained window at the back of the hall, just enough to show outlines as Ned felt his way towards the head of the stairs. But there was one question Eve had to ask.

All her life she had been trying to avoid unpleasant things. She wanted to avoid the unpleasantness, perhaps even the horror, which rose like a human face behind the image of Maurice Lawes battered to death with a poker in the gimcrack room of white walls and spindly gilt furniture. But this time it could not be avoided. It suggested possibilities which might touch her life too closely. She thought of the big clock in the tower of the town hall, which housed the prefecture of police. She thought of M. Goron, the prefect. She thought of a gray morning and a chopping guillotine.

"Ned. It *was* a burglar, wasn't it?"

"That's damned funny," he said abruptly.

"What is?"

"When I came up here tonight, this hall was as black as your hat. I'll swear the curtain wasn't drawn on that window." He pointed towards the back of the hall. As he reflected, belief grew to conviction in his mind. "I stumbled on the stairs. On that rod. And, if there had been any light, I shouldn't have stumbled. Just what the blazes is going on here?"

"Ned Atwood, you're not going to put me off like that! It *was* a burglar, wasn't it?"

He drew a deep breath.

"No, old girl. You know it wasn't."

"I won't believe you! Whatever it is, I won't believe it!"

"Angel, don't be a damned fool." He spoke blank-
ly. She could see his eyes, almost luminous in the
gloom. "It never occurred to me that I, of all people,
should wind up as a protector of the weak. But you,
my wench . . . *you* . . . !"

"What about me?"

"You oughtn't to be out alone, that's all."

The steep, curving staircase below them was a pit
of darkness. Ned put his hand on the banister rail as
though he wanted to shake it loose.

"I've been trying to decide whether I ought to tell
you, or oughtn't to." He closed his fist and spoke with
toiling lucidity. "I hate getting mixed up with the
morals of things; and I don't mean sexual morals
either. You see — it's just occurred to me that this
situation isn't new. I once gave it the horse-laugh
myself, when I heard about it happening in Victorian
times."

"What on earth are you talking about?"

"Don't you remember? The story was started
nearly a hundred years ago, at the time Lord William
Somebody was murdered by his valet."

"But poor Maurice hasn't got a valet."

"If you don't stop being so literal-minded, angel,"
said Ned, "I'm going to put you across my knee and

smack you. Haven't you ever heard the yarn?"

"No."

"The murder was supposed to have been witnessed by a man standing at the window of the house opposite. Only he couldn't speak out and denounce the murderer, because *he* was in the bedroom of a married woman where he had no business to be. So, when they arrested an innocent man for the murder, what was he going to do?

"Of course, the story's a myth. There never was any doubt about the identity of the murderer in that particular case. But the story's been handed down, because people got all excited about the predicament of that sedate Victorian couple who'd been up to funny business and yet couldn't admit it. *I* always thought it was a kind of comic situation — until now."

After a pause he added:

"But it's not funny. It's not funny at all."

"Ned, who did it? Who killed him?"

Her companion seemed so engrossed in the old problem that he did not hear her question about the new one. Perhaps he did not want to hear.

"If I remember rightly, somebody wrote a play about it."

"Ned, for heaven's sake!"

"No, listen to me! This is important!" She saw his

white face in the gloom. "In the play, they just dodged the issue. The poor mug wrote an anonymous letter to the police, denouncing the murderer, and seemed to think that settled everything. Of course it didn't settle anything. The only way they could actually have got out of the difficulty would have been to stand up in open court and testify against the real murderer."

At the ominous word "court," Eve again seized at his arm. But he reassured her. He had taken one step down the stairs. Now he turned to face her. The studied muttering of their voices, expressing the need for frantic hurry in people who did not hurry, grew lower and lower as it grew more fierce.

"Don't worry. You won't be involved. I'll see to that."

"You're not going to tell the police?"

"I'm not going to tell anybody."

"But you can tell me. Who did it?"

He shook off her hand and took another step down. He was walking backwards, his left hand on the banister rail. His face, a whitish blur which showed a gleam of teeth, seemed to recede away from her into mist.

The thought which flashed through Eve's mind was so ugly that only overwrought nerves could have put it there.

"No," corrected Ned, with that infuriating habit of reading her mind. "Don't fret yourself about that, either. It wasn't anybody in the household that you need trouble yourself over."

"You swear that?"

"Yes," replied Ned. "I swear just exactly that."

"Are you trying to torture me?"

Ned spoke very quietly.

"On the contrary, I'm trying to keep you wrapped in cotton-wool. That's where you belong. That's where all your men try to keep you. But, by the Lord Harry! — for a gal of your age and presumed experience, you've got more dewy-eyed illusions about the sweet simplicity of the world than anybody I ever did see! All right." He drew a deep breath. "You may as well hear about it sooner or later."

"Hurry, please!"

"The first time we looked across there . . . remember?"

Try as she might to shut it out, the picture always returned. With Ned's eyes on her, she saw again the big table-desk against the left-hand wall, and Papa Lawes with his magnifying glass and little tuft of chin whisker, as she had seen him so many times before the head wore a cap of blood. Now a shadow hovered over it, distorting the outlines.

"The first time we looked across, I said I thought

there was somebody with the old man. But I couldn't tell who it was."

"Well?"

"But the second time, when all the lights were on . . ."

Eve had taken one step down the stairs after him. She did not mean to reach out and give him a violent shove. It was the sudden shrilling of the police-whistle that did the damage.

Out in the street, that whistle was blowing with an insistence which cried murder, and summoned every agent within hearing distance on a view-halloo after a non-existent burglar. The note of the whistle quivered up again, plainly heard through open windows. What Eve felt, in the blind shock of hearing it, was merely a frantic desire to hurry him downstairs: to fling him away, to rid herself of dangers by physically propelling him out of the house. Her hands were on Ned's shoulders, and she pushed.

He did not even have time to cry out. He was balanced precariously, his back to the stair-well, his heel over the edge of the tread, and his left hand resting lightly on the banister rail. He lost his grip, staggered, uttered an angry grunt, and took one step backwards — full on the loose stair rod below. She saw his stupid, staring expression for the fraction of a second before he fell.

V

A human body, flung and bounced down sixteen steps of a breakneck staircase, to end by striking its head full against the wall at the foot of the stairs, might be thought to make a noise capable of shaking the house.

Actually, Eve could afterwards remember very little noise. This may have been due to shock, or she may have been expecting a din so shattering that her own nerves deafened her. To her there seemed scarcely a break between the time Ned fell and the time she was bending over him, panting, at the foot of the stairs.

She had meant no harm. It never occurred to her that a good-looking, good-natured woman, who combines gentle manners with more sex-appeal than is good for her, can be suspected of sinister motives no matter what she does. She knew, of course, that she lived in dread of scandal. But she never went on to analyze why the brush of scandal never kept very far from her skirts. It just seemed to happen to her.

Eve's conscience was at her again. Fully convinced

that she must have killed Ned Atwood, she had never been closer to loving him. The hall below, where the stairs curved, was so dark that she stumbled over his body. This seemed the fitting end to a nightmare, a time when she might as well open the front door and call for the police to end it. She could have wept with relief when the apparent corpse stirred and spoke.

"What damn monkey tricks do you think you're playing? Why did you push me?"

The wave of relief passed like a wave of nausea.

"Can you get up? Are you hurt?"

"No, of course I'm not hurt. Bit shaken up, though. I s-say, what happened?"

"Sh-h!"

He seemed to be sprawled on his hands and knees, swaying a little, before he could push himself to his feet. His voice sounded almost normal, if rather uncertain. Bending over him, struggling to help him up, Eve touched his face and ran her hands across his hair; and her hands recoiled from the wet stickiness of blood.

"You're hurt!"

"Nonsense! Bit shaken up, that's all. Feel funny, though. Shoulder feels funny. Cripes, what a tumble. Look here, why did you push me?"

"Darling, there's blood on your face! Have you got a match? Or a lighter? Strike it!"

There was a slight pause. "Blood's from my nose. I can feel it. Funny, too. Didn't seem to hit my nose; at least, it feels all right. Got a lighter. Here."

The tiny flame of the lighter sprang up. Taking it out of his hand while he fumbled with a handkerchief, she held it high to look at him. There seemed to be nothing wrong with him, though his hair was rumpled and his coat dusty. His nose had been bleeding; Eve felt a twitch of repulsion at the blood on her own hand. But he easily stanched this, and replaced the handkerchief in his pocket. His crushed hat he picked up, dusted, and put on.

All this while Ned's face looked faintly sullen and puzzled. Several times he licked at his lips and swallowed, as though testing a taste he could not account for. He kept shaking his head and flexing his shoulders, experimentally. The face was rather pale, the blue eyes blank and puckered up as though with concentration.

"Are you *sure* you're all right?"

"I'm perfectly fit, thanks." He snatched the lighter out of her hand and extinguished it. It was a flash of that furious, diabolical temper he had shown in the past. "Queer. Very queer. And, now that you've tried to murder me, will you for the love of Christ let me get out of here?"

Yes. This was the old Ned Atwood. It was a ghost

which terrified her. For a while, there, she had almost thought . . .

In silence they crept out through the dark villa to
the back door in the kitchen. Eve unfastened its
spring lock. From here, a few stone steps led up into
a little rustic garden surrounded by the high stone
wall. A back gate in this wall led you into a lane
which in turn communicated with the Boulevard du
Casino.

The back door creaked in an utter hush. Warm air
lay drowsy on the eyelids, full of a scent of damp
grass and the perfume of roses. Far away over the
roofs, the beam of the great inland lighthouse dazzled
and then died, once every twenty seconds. They
stood for a moment at the foot of the steps leading
up into the garden. From the front, Eve could now
hear a babble of voices in the street which indicated
that the police had arrived.

She spoke close to his ear, in a fierce whisper. "Ned,
wait. You were going to tell me who . . ."

"Good night," said Mr. Atwood courteously.

He bent forward, and in a perfunctory and absent-
minded manner kissed her on the lips. Again she felt
a faint splash of blood. He touched his hat to her,
turned round, ascended the steps with a slight stag-
ger, but walked steadily across the yard to the gate.

Eve did not dare call out after him, though all her

fears and energies boiled up into a kind of stifled shriek. She ran up the steps, the sash band of her negligée drooping loose again, and made frantic gestures which he did not even notice. This was why she failed to hear the slight click of the back door.

Once he was out of the house, she had thought, the danger would be over. She could breathe again; she could rid herself of this stifling fear of discovery.

But things weren't returning to normal. Eve was conscious of a vague fright arising from a source she could not name. But it clung round Ned Atwood. From the grinning, lounging boy she had known, Ned had been changed as though by magic into a courteous stranger, detached and a trifle eerie. He would be all right in the morning, no doubt. But in the morning . . .

Eve drew a deep breath. She crept back down the stairs again. She put out her hand to the door, and stopped dead. The door had swung shut. Its spring lock was now fastened on the inside.

To every person on this earth, there sometimes comes a day when every single thing goes wrong — and from no discoverable cause. To most women it comes oftener than that. She may begin, mildly, by breaking the eggs she is frying for breakfast: hardly a catastrophe, yet hateful to the feminine soul. Then she breaks something in the drawing room. Afterwards it is all trouble. Household perplexities, which may have slept for weeks like snakes in cold weather, suddenly awake and sting. When even inanimate objects seem possessed by malignant demons, her frustrated anger cannot break out except in the bewildered feeling: "What have I done to *deserve* this?"

That was how Eve felt, when she tugged fiercely at the knob of the door which had blown shut.

And yet . . .

How could the door have blown shut?

There was not a breath of wind. Though the night seemed chillier than she had thought, nothing moved or stirred under the clear stars and the trees of the garden.

That didn't matter now. If some devilish horoscope had decreed that all these things were to happen to her at once, it was no good asking how. It simply happened. What she must decide was how to get back in again. At any moment the police might come nosing and find her.

Bang on the door?

And arouse Yvette? The thought of Yvette's strong, unimpassioned face, with its shiny little black eyes and eyebrows that met in the middle like sparse fur, caused in her a revulsion which was like rage. Admit it: she was terrified of Yvette, though she could not in the least understand why. But how to get in? The windows were no good: the ground-floor windows, each night, were locked and shuttered on the inside.

Eve put her hands to her forehead; and, becoming once more aware of the wet stickiness of blood, snatched them away again. Her night clothes must be a sight. She tried to look at them, but the light was too dim. It was in plucking at her negligée, holding it out in front of her with a comparatively clean left hand, that she found in the pocket of her pajamas Ned Atwood's key to the front door.

One side of her mind cried: The street's full of policemen! You can't go round to the front! The other side whispered that, after all, there was the stone wall of the villa itself to shield her from being seen from the street. She could slip round the side of the house; and, if she made no noise, she might be able to whip through the front door without attracting attention.

It was some time before Eve could make up her mind. Feeling more and more undressed with each passing second, she finally essayed it at a run. She kept close to the house. Breathing hard, she emerged into the front garden — and came face to face with Toby Lawes.

He couldn't see her, of course. That was the only piece of luck so far.

They *were* looking for her, as she had predicted. Toby, wearing a long raincoat over pajamas and shoes, had crossed the street and was just putting his hand on the gate of the Villa Miramar.

The wall fronting the street was perhaps nine feet high, its entrance an arched opening with an iron-grilled gate. The tall, dim street lamps of the rue des Anges made a spectral green glow against the branches of chestnut trees; they threw the front garden of Eve's house into shadow, and illuminated Toby's figure outside the gate. Nor was the rue des Anges full of policemen. On the contrary, it was one officious agent who saved Eve from discovery. As Toby reached the gate, an excited voice thundered out behind him.

"*Attendez là, jeune homme!*" the voice shouted. "*Qu'est-ce je vois? Vous partez à l'anglais, hein? Hein, hein, HEIN?*"

The whirlwind of rattling syllables mounted with each "hein." Footsteps came pounding across the street.

Toby swung round, spreading out his hands, and replied in French. His French was fluent, though he spoke with an execrable accent which Eve often suspected he deliberately cultivated so as to show no concessions to any damned foreigners.

"I go only," he shouted back, "to the house

of Madame Neill. Here!" He thumped the gate.

"No, monsieur. It is not permitted to leave the house. You will return, please. Quick, quick, quick!"

"But, I tell you —!"

"Return, please. No stupidities, if you please!"

Toby made a gesture of weary exasperation. Eve saw him swing round under the light: she saw, through bars, the good-humored countenance with its cropped mustache and brown woolly hair now strained and tautened by an emotion so strong that it seemed to bewilder him. Toby lifted his fists. That he was suffering horribly could not have been doubted by anybody, least of all by Eve.

"Monsieur the inspector," he said, and it must be remembered that the French *inspecteur* merely means policeman, "will you have the kindness to remember my mother? She is having hysterics upstairs. You saw her."

"Ah!" said the law.

"She wishes me to find Madame Neill. Madame Neill is the only one who can help her. Besides, I am not taking English leave. I am only going here." And he began to whack the gate again.

"You are going nowhere, monsieur."

"My father is dead . . ."

"And is it my fault," snapped the law, "if an assassination is done here? An assassination in La Bandelette! That goes too far! What M. Goron will say I do not like to think. Suicides at the Casino — that is bad enough. But this!" Then the hoarse voice rose in despair. "Oh, my God, another of them!"

This anguish was inspired by the fact that another set of footsteps, quick light footsteps this time, came rapping across the street. Janice Lawes, in vivid scarlet pajamas, joined the two by the gate. Her fluffy light-red hair, worn in a long bob, contrasted with the pajamas and with the dead pallor of her pretty face. Janice at twenty-three was small and round, trim and trig, bouncing and assertive, with an eighteenth-century kind of figure and (sometimes) an eighteenth-century demureness. Just now she looked dazed and ready to scream.

"What's wrong?" she cried to Toby. "Where's Eve? Why are you standing there?"

"Because this fathead says . . ."

"Are you letting that stop you? *I* shouldn't."

The law evidently understood English. As Janice looked through the bars of the gate — straight into Eve's eyes without seeing her — another blast of a police whistle made all their scalps tingle.

"That is for my friends," the agent said grimly. "Now, then, monsieur! Now, then, mademoiselle! Will you come back with me quietly, or will you be escorted?"

He came dancing into Eve's sight, and laid hold of Toby's arm. From under his cloak he had whipped out a short white hard-rubber truncheon, which he turned over in his hand.

"Monsieur!" His blast became plaintive. "I regret! This is not pleasant for me. Nor is it pleasant for you, to see your father like that."

Toby put his hands over his eyes. Janice suddenly turned and ran back towards their own house.

"But I have my orders! Come, now!" The agent's voice had a hollow, not unsympathetic wheedle of persuasion. "It is not so bad, is it? A little quarter of an hour until the director arrives! One little quarter of an hour! Then you may see her, without the least doubt. Hein? In the meantime, if you please . . ."

"All right," Toby said despondently.

The policeman released his arm. Toby cast one glance at the Villa Miramar before he left. An incongruous figure in the long raincoat, square-jawed and stocky, he spoke unexpectedly. He had lost all sense of the proprieties. His emotion was so strong that he sounded wildly melodramatic.

"Finest, sweetest-natured person that ever lived!" he said.

"Eh?"

"Madame Neill," explained Toby, and pointed.

"Ah!" said the law, craning round for a glance at this paragon's house.

"Nothing like her," said Toby. "Never has been. High-thinking and pure and sweet and . . ." He gulped, controlling himself with so fierce an effort that Eve could almost feel it. "If I am not permitted to go there," he added in French, turning reddish eyes towards the gate, "would there be any objection if I telephoned to her?"

"My orders, monsieur," replied the law, after a slight pause, "do not include telephones. Yes. One may telephone. Faith, now, it is not necessary to run!"

Telephones again.

Eve prayed that the agent would not stay where he was, peering through the gate. She must beat Toby Lawes to the phone, and be there when it rang. She had never realized so clearly how much Toby idealized her. She could have walloped his ears for such high-flown nonsense. Yet it made her heart ache in a new, queer way. While one part of her mind fumed with impatience, yet the essential feminine —that side which almost exults in self-sacrifice — swore again that she would do anything rather than let Toby learn about this messy interlude of tonight.

The policeman, after opening the gate, sticking his head inside, and causing Eve to stop breathing for several seconds, seemed satisfied. She heard his footsteps cross the street. The door of the house opposite closed with a slam. Eve ducked her head and ran for her own front door.

In a vague way it occurred to her that the negligée was flying; that the waistband had come loose once more. She paid no attention. Only a few running steps separated her from the front door. It seemed to her an endless, eternal void, a wild gauntlet running in which at any moment she might be caught and struck dead. Even putting the key in the lock seemed to take an eternity, while the lock eluded her and the flanges of the key rasped and wavered without taking hold.

Then she was inside, in the warm and welcome dark. The soft thud of the closing door shut her away from devils. She had made it, and she felt — which was quite true — that nobody had seen her. Eve's heart was thudding; the blood on her hand felt moist again; her wits seemed to turn round as on a slow wheel. While she stood crouched in the dark, getting her breath back again, smoothing out her mind and emotions so that she could talk sanely to Toby, the telephone commenced to ring upstairs.

She needn't fear that now. Everything, she told herself, would come out right. Of course everything would come out right. Everything *must* come out right. She drew her negligée more closely round her, and crept upstairs to answer the telephone.

VI

It was just a week later — on the afternoon of Monday, September first — that M. Aristide Goron sat on the terrace of the Donjon Hotel with his friend Dr. Dermot Kinross.

M. Goron made a face.

"We have arranged," he confided, stirring his coffee, "to arrest Madame Eve Neill for the murder of Sir Maurice Lawes."

"There is no doubt about the evidence?"

"Unhappily, none."

Dermot Kinross felt a shiver, "Will she be . . . ?"

M. Goron considered. "No," he decided, half closing one eye as though watching a scales, "I think it very unlikely. That is a soft neck, a handsome neck."

"Well?"

"Fifteen years on the island: that is most probable. Ten years perhaps, or even five, if she has a clever lawyer and makes good use of her charms. Of course, you understand, even five years on the island is not a bag of shells."

"God knows it isn't. And how is Madame Neill — taking this?"

M. Goron fidgeted.

"Dear doctor," he said, taking the spoon out of his coffee cup and putting it down, "that is the worst of it! This charming lady thinks she has got away with it. She has not the remotest idea that she is even suspected! When it becomes my very painful duty to tell her . . ."

If the prefect of police was pained, he had reason for it. Crime, rare in La Bandelette, distressed him. M. Goron was a comfortable man, a round, amiable, catlike sort of man, with spats and a white rose in his buttonhole. The duties of a prefect are seldom those of a policeman: he acted as a sort of master of ceremonies to La Bandelette. But M. Goron was also a shrewd man.

Round him stretched his domain, the white Avenue de la Forêt asparkle with cars and open carriages in the late afternoon sunlight. Above was the façade of the Donjon Hotel, whose striped orange-and-black awnings shut away the sun from the terrace. There were not many persons sitting at the little tables. M. Goron's rather protruding eyes regarded his guest fixedly.

"Yet she is wretched, this Madame Neill!" he added. "Something terrifies her. She has only to look at this Lawes family, and she becomes a different person. Is it conscience, I ask myself? Or what? As I say, the evidence is complete . . ."

"And yet," said Dermot Kinross in pretty fair French, "you are not satisfied."

M. Goron's eyes narrowed.

"That is clever of you," he conceded. "In candor: no. I am not *altogether* satisfied. Therefore I have a favor to ask of you."

Dermot returned his bland smile.

It would have been difficult to say wherein lay Dr. Kinross's air of distinction, so that you singled him out in a crowd and thought he might be an interesting person to know. It was perhaps the essential tolerance of the face, the suggestion that he was the same sort of person you were yourself, and would understand you.

It was a weather-beaten face, kindly and absent-minded, a little lined by study, with absent-minded dark eyes. There was still no gray in the thick dark hair. You would not have guessed — except at certain angles — that one side of this face had been rebuilt by plastic surgery after a shell-burst at Arras. Humor you saw there, and wisdom without flippancy; but strength you never saw until it was needed.

He smoked a cigarette, and had a whiskey-and-soda at his elbow. Though he seemed in a holiday mood, he had never in his life known what a holiday meant.

"Continue," he said.

The prefect of police lowered his voice.

"Now here, you would have said, was a perfect match. I mean Madame Eve Neill and Monsieur . . . they call him Tobee, but his name is Horatio . . . Lawes. An ideal match, with money in it. Almost a grand passion."

"There is no such thing," observed Dermot Kinross, "as a grand passion. Nature has arranged that if A had never met B he would have been just as happy with C."

M. Goron regarded him with polite skepticism.

"You believe that, doctor?"

"I know it as a scientific fact."

"Then I take it," said M. Goron, remaining politely skeptical, "that you have never met Madame Neill?"

"No," smiled Dermot. "But my failure to meet a certain lady can hardly be said to alter a scientific fact."

"Ah, well!" sighed M. Goron, and got down to business. "One week ago tonight, the household at the Villa Bonheur in the rue des Anges consisted of Sir Maurice Lawes, his lady, his daughter Janice, his son M. Horatio, and his brother-in-law M. Benjamin Phillips. There were, in addition, two servants.

"At eight o'clock Madame Neill, and all the Lawes family except Sir Maurice, departed for the theatre.

Sir Maurice refused to go. He had seemed in a very queer temper — mark that! — ever since his return from his usual afternoon walk. But this temper changed. At half-past eight he was rung up on the telephone by his friend M. Veille, the art dealer of the rue de la Harpe. M. Veille reported that he had acquired a jewel, a treasure, a stunning addition for Sir Maurice's collection. M. Veille suggested that he should bring this marvel to the Villa Bonheur for Sir Maurice's immediate inspection. And this he did."

M. Goron paused. Dr. Dermot Kinross blew up smoke, watching it curl in the warm lazy air.

"And the nature of this treasure?" he asked.

"It was a snuff-box," answered M. Goron. "A snuff-box said to have belonged to the Emperor Napoleon himself."

The prefect of police looked bewildered.

"When M. Veille later told me the price of this article," he went on, "I could not believe him. Sacred name! What people will pay for fads! Of course, apart from its historic interest . . ." He hesitated, craftily. "A propos! I suppose the Emperor Napoleon really did take snuff?"

Dermot laughed.

"My friend," he said, "have you ever seen the part of Napoleon played on the English stage? No actor would think of playing it for five minutes without juggling a snuff-box and hurling it all over the stage at every third speech. Even in authentic memoirs he is always spilling snuff over himself."

M. Goron frowned.

"There seems no reason," he conceded, "to doubt the authenticity of the article. But its intrinsic value!" He drank coffee and rolled up his eyes. "It was made—look!—of transparent rose agate, bound with gold and set in small diamonds. Of curious shape, as you shall see. It carries with it a written pedigree, guaranteeing its genuineness.

"Sir Maurice was delighted. It appears that he had a fondness for Napoleonic relics. He agreed to buy the box, asking leave to keep it now and saying that he would send a check in the morning. Incidentally, the box is still unpaid for and M. Veille is having fits and, faith, I don't blame him.

"On the same night Madame Neill, as I told you, went to the theatre with the rest of the Lawes family. The piece they saw was an English play called *Mrs. Varren's Profession*. They returned home at about eleven o'clock, and there they separated. Young M. Horatio Lawes escorts her to her door, where he leaves her. Later, by the way, the examining magistrate asks him: 'Monsieur, did you kiss her goodnight?' The young man draws himself up like a stuffed owl and sternly answers: 'Monsieur, that is no business of yours.' Which the examining magistrate thought very suspicious, as perhaps indicating a quarrel. But it appears there was nothing of the kind."

Again M. Goron hesitated.

"The Lawes family return to their villa. There they are greeted by Sir Maurice, who comes rushing downstairs to show them this treasure, in a little green-and-gold case. They display — with the exception of little Miss Janice, who says it is beautiful — a singular lack of enthusiasm. Lady Lawes declares it is a sinful waste of money. Sir Maurice Lawes, in something of a huff, pointedly says he will retire to his study where he can get some peace. The rest of them go to bed.

"But two of them, observe, are unable to sleep."

M. Goron leaned over and tapped the table. He was so engrossed in the recital that his coffee had grown cold.

"M. Horatio, this Tobee, admits he must rise up at one o'clock in the morning and telephone to Madame Neill. 'Ah!' says the examining magistrate; 'you were on fire with love, no doubt?' Whereat M. Horatio changes color and denies that he is on fire with anything. Not a clue, true! But, palpably, there is an atmosphere here. Something in the air. You agree?"

"Not necessarily," said Dermot.

M. Goron blinked at him.

"You do not agree?"

"Never mind that, for the moment. Go on."

"*Alors*! He goes downstairs to telephone, returns, and goes to bed. The house is dark. He hears no sound. He sees a light under the door of his father's study, but does not disturb Sir Maurice.

"At the same time, Lady Lawes herself is restless. She is not exactly distressed or upset over the purchase of this snuff-box. But it worries her a little. She cannot sleep. At a quarter past one in the morning —— mark the time! — *she* rises. She goes to her husband's study. Ostensibly to beg him to come to bed; but really, as she confesses, to preach a mild sermon about people who buy such expensive bits of rose agate."

M. Goron's voice raised and sharpened like an actor's.

"Finish!" he said, suddenly snapping his fingers. "She finds him sitting dead at his desk.

"His head has been beaten in by nine blows from a poker which now hangs in a stand of fire irons across the room. He has been sitting with his back to the room, writing a description of the snuff-box which we find on a writing pad before him. But more! One of the blows, either by accident or design, has landed on the agate snuff-box and smashed it to bits."

Dermot whistled.

"It is not enough," said M. Goron, "to take the old man's life. His treasure must be destroyed as well. Or perhaps (I repeat) it was an accident."

Dermot was growing more and more disturbed.

"You could hardly aim at a target like a man's head," he replied, "and hit a snuff-box on a desk in front of him. Unless, of course . . ."

"You were saying, dear doctor?"

"Nothing. Please go on."

M. Goron had half risen on the tips of his toes, hand cupped behind his ear, as though to catch words of wisdom. His rather protruding eyes were fixed on Dermot. But he sank back again.

"This crime," he pursued, "is brutal. It is senseless. On the surface, it is almost the work of a madman . . ."

"Nonsense," said Dermot, with slight irritation. "On the contrary, it is absolutely characteristic."

"*Characteristic?*"

"Of its type, yes. Forgive my interrupting you. Go on."

"Nothing is stolen," said M. Goron. "There are no signs of burglarious entry. This crime has been committed by someone who knows the house, knows that a poker hangs by the fireplace, and even knows that the old man is slightly deaf so that he may be approached unheard from behind. This Lawes family is a happy household, almost French. I assure you! Properly, they are bewildered and they are horrified."

"And then?"

"They go to seek Madame Neill. They are fond of Madame Neill. Immediately after the crime is discovered, I am told, both M. Horatio and Miss Janice made determined efforts to see her. They were stopped by the policeman in charge, who properly told them they must not leave the house until the commissaire of police had arrived. I have even heard that Miss Janice slipped out of the house once more. But evidently she did not see Madame Neill.

"The commissaire arrives. Good! He questions them. Good! They ask if they may see Madame Neill. The commissaire offers to send a man across the street to fetch her. This man, the same agent of police who has already shown such zeal, is despatched on the errand. By good luck, he carries a light. The houses are just opposite, as you may have heard or read . . . ?"

"Yes," admitted Dermot.

"The agent," said M. Goron, leaning both fat elbows on the table and screwing up his face hideously, "opens the gate and goes up the path. In the path, just outside the front door of Madame Neill's villa, he finds . . ."

"Well?" prompted the other, as M. Goron paused.

"A pink satin band or belt, such as women wear round dressing-gowns or negligées. And it is slightly stained with blood."

"I see."

Again there was a pause.

"But this agent, he is cunning. He puts the satin band in his pocket, and says nothing. He rings the doorbell. Presently it is answered by two frightened women. The names of these women are," — here M. Goron took out a very tiny memorandum book, which he held up to peer at, — "Yvette Latour, madame's personal maid. And Célestine Bouchère, the cook.

"These women whisper to him from the dark. They have their fingers at their lips. They enjoin silence. They draw him into a downstairs room, and explain what they have seen.

"Yvette Latour tells how she is waked up by much noise. She goes out of her room, and sees Madame Neill creeping back into the house. Alarmed (though this is a strong-minded woman), Yvette wakes up Célestine Bouchère the cook. They creep down and peep into Madame Neill's bedroom. Beyond, in a bathroom walled with looking-glasses, they see Madame Neill, much toussled and breathing from hard exertion, engaged in washing blood from her hands and face, and attempting to sponge out smaller blood spots from a white lace negligée whose waistband is missing."

M. Goron glanced quickly over his shoulder.

More people were drifting along the terrace of the Donjon Hotel. The sun, sinking beyond the pine forest at the other side of the Avenue de la Forêt, was now in their eyes.

It was, Dermot Kinross thought, a picture of almost intolerable vividness: the furtiveness, the peering servants, the agitated face multiplied by mirrors. It came from the dark night of evil, which was the province of the police, but also from the dark night of the mind, which was his own province. For the moment, he suspended judgment. He only said:

"And then?"

"Well! Our agent swears the two servants, Yvette and Célestine, to absolute silence. He goes upstairs boldly and knocks at Madame Neill's bedroom door."

"She was in bed?"

"On the contrary," returned M. Goron, with a breath of admiration, "she was dressing herself in outdoor clothes. She explained that M. Horatio Lawes had awakened her with a telephone call — *another* telephone call, you observe, only a few minutes before — to tell her of the tragedy. Previous to that, she says she has heard nothing. Not police whistles or shouting in the street. Nothing!

"But, dear doctor! My God, what acting! How she is shocked to tears by the death of Sir Maurice Lawes! How her lips open! How her eyes widen! There is the innocence of the pink rose, eh? And the white negligée hangs up in the wardrobe; and, in the bathroom adjoining, there is still steam on the mirrors from her efforts to wash away the old man's blood."

Dermot stirred uncomfortably.

"What about your policeman? What did he do?"

"He laughed up his sleeve, kept a face of iron, and asked her if she would have the kindness to come across the street and comfort her friends. Then he made an excuse to lag behind."

"In order to . . . ?"

"Exactly. In order to take possession, in secret, of the negligée."

"Well?"

"Yvette the maid was enjoined to say, under horrible oaths of silence, that it had been sent to the cleaner's when Madame next asked for it. Several other things were genuinely sent to the cleaner's to preserve the fiction. Would Madame care? No! The few blood spots were washed out. Of course, that such stains are always present for chemical examination undoubtedly never occurred to her. But the blood spots, dear doctor, are not at all the most interesting thing about that negligée."

"No?"

"No," said M. Goron, and drummed on the table. "It is Yvette Latour who closely examines that robe under the eyes of my man. It is Yvette Latour who finds, clinging to the lace, a small sliver of rose agate."

This time the prefect of police's pause was not one of drama. It was one of deep and regretful finality.

"A week of patient reconstruction has enabled us to fit that sliver exactly into its place in the shattered snuff-box. It was a chip which flew wide from the box when Madame Eve Neill took a poker and beat the old man to death. This is a devilish thing. But it is conclusive. It serves. And it will end Madame Neill's public career, I think."

There was a silence. Dermot cleared his throat.

"What explanation," he inquired, "has Madame Neill for all this?"

M. Goron looked shocked.

"I beg your pardon," Dermot added. "I forgot. You haven't mentioned it to her yet, have you?"

"In this country, doctor," — M. Goron spoke with dignity, — "we do not consider it good sense to show our cards until the game is complete. She will be asked for explanations. But that will come after the arrest, when she is confronted with the examining magistrate."

And very unpleasant things, Dermot remembered, those confrontations could be. Though no actual third-degree was employed, the law permitted nearly every form of "mental" pressure. It would require a very tough, very strong-minded woman to outface her questioners and say nothing she might afterwards regret.

"Are you sure," he asked, "that no word of your evidence against Madame Neill has leaked out?"

"Very sure, monsieur."

"I congratulate you. What about the two servants, Yvette Latour and Célestine Bouchère? Do they gossip?"

"No: that arranges itself. Célestine has been sent away for the moment, pleading shock. The other one, the maid, has been a tower of strength. She keeps her mouth shut." M. Goron looked thoughtful. "And I do not think she likes Madame Neill very much."

"So?"

"But one thing I can tell you. This Lawes family have been magnificent! It is impossible to admire them too much. They are nearly out of their minds.

Yet they answer all our questions. They keep what you call," for three words M. Goron ventured into English, "the steef ooper leep. They are tirelessly kind to Madame Neill. . . ."

"And why shouldn't they be? Do they suspect her of the murder?"

"Sacred name, no!"

"How do *they* account for the murder, then?"

M. Goron waved his hands. "How can they account for it? A burglar! A maniac!"

"Yet nothing was stolen?"

"Nothing," M. Goron conceded, "was stolen. But something else besides the agate snuff-box was disturbed. In a glass case to the left of the door in the old man's study was another treasure of his collection. This was a valuable diamond-and-turquoise necklace, also with a historical pedigree."

"Well?"

"The necklace, slightly bloodstained, was found flung down in a heap under the curio cabinet afterwards. A maniac!"

Dr. Dermot Kinross, who was perhaps the foremost mental specialist in England on the subject of criminal psychology, looked across at his companion with a curious expression.

"A convenient term," he said.

"A convenient term, dear doctor? What?"

" 'Maniac.' How was this alleged burgling maniac supposed to have got into the house?"

"That, fortunately," said M. Goron, "is a point which has not yet occurred to the family."

"If it comes to that, how did Madame Neill herself get into it?"

M. Goron sighed.

"I fear," he said, "that it is the final proof. Four of the villas in the rue des Anges were put up by the same building company. The keys of one will fit the doors of all the others."

Again with reluctant weightiness, M. Goron leaned across the table.

"In the breast pocket of Madame Neill's pajamas," he went on, "the invaluable Yvette Latour discovered a key to the front door of her own villa. Now, come! A key to one's *own* villa, carried in the *pajamas*? For what purpose? Can you think of any reasonable explanation — any innocent explanation — why you keep such a key on your person when you are ready for bed? No. There is only one explanation. Madame Neill needed it to get into the house across the street. It constitutes the final contributing proof that she visited the Villa Bonheur on the night of the murder."

They had got her. No doubt about that.

"Still . . . the woman's motive?" Dermot persisted.

And M. Goron told him.

The sun had dipped behind the trees across the avenue. Pink fire remained in the sky, a mild and heady warmth in the air. French sunshine can be as blinding as a spotlight; when its dazzle left their eyes, they blinked to adjust themselves to it. A small bead of sweat remained on M. Goron's forehead.

Dermot got up to throw the stump of his cigarette over the stone balustrade by which they had been sitting. But he did not throw it. His hand remained in the air.

The terrace was raised perhaps two or three feet above the level of the ground below, a graveled court dotted with little tables like those of the terrace. At a table close against the balustrade, her head about on a.level with their feet, sat a girl whose dark dress and hat stood out sombrely against the color of La Bandelette. Her head was raised; Dermot was looking straight into her eyes.

She was a pretty girl of twenty-two or three, he noticed. She had light red hair. How long she had been sitting there, concealed by sunlight, he could not guess. An untasted cocktail stood in front of her. Beyond her moved the humming, hooting cars of the Avenue de la Forêt, soothed by the lazier noise of open carriages which clopped and jingled past as though nothing had happened or could ever happen.

Suddenly the girl jumped to her feet. Her side knocked against the little orange-topped table, upsetting the cocktail glass with a clatter into its saucer, and splashing its contents wide. The girl snatched up a handbag and a pair of openwork black gloves. She threw a five-franc piece on the table; then she turned and ran out into the street. Dermot stood staring after her, remembering the expression of her eyes.

M. Goron spoke softly.

"Curse and condemn to the eternal fires all conversations in public places!" he swore. "That was Miss Janice Lawes."

VII

"NONSENSE, my dear Janice," soothed Helena. "You're hysterical."

The mildly shocked and harassed expression on the face of Uncle Ben, as he leaned over to ruffle the ears of the King Charles spaniel beside the tea wagon, was comment enough on his part.

"I'm not hysterical," returned Janice in a low, rapid voice which showed she was not far off it. She stripped off her gloves. "And I'm not dreaming and I'm not guessing and I'm not imagining things. I tell you," — her voice went up; she glanced briefly at Eve without meeting her eye, — "they're coming to arrest Eve!"

Helena blinked.

"But why?"

"Mother dear, because they think she did it!"

"What tiresome nonsense you do pick up," sighed Helena. But there was a startled, wondering silence just the same.

This couldn't be happening, Eve thought to herself. It wasn't possible. It was the one possibility she had never even dreamed of.

Mechanically Eve put down her tea cup. The drawing room at the Villa Bonheur was long and spacious, with a polished hardwood floor. Its windows in front faced the rue des Anges; its windows at the rear admitted a green, cool twilight from the big garden. There was the tea wagon, and the shaggy golden-brown spaniel raising his big eyes to Uncle Ben. There was Uncle Ben himself, a middle-sized stocky man with short grizzled hair and a taciturn but smiling expression. There was Helena, stout and amiable and short of breath, her silver-white bobbed hair contrasting with the round rosy face which now wore a fixed and incredulous smile.

And here was Janice, saying. . .

Janice seemed to be nerving herself for a strong effort. She looked straight at Eve.

"Listen, Eve," she said piteously, and moistened her lips. Janice had rather a large mouth, which did not detract from the prettiness of her face. "We know you *didn't*, of course."

She spoke with a sort of desperate apology. And she could not look at Eve any longer.

"But why should they —" began Helena.

"Suspect —" continued Uncle Ben.

"All the same," Janice continued, with her eyes fixed on the mirror over the mantelpiece, "you *weren't* out that night, were you? You *didn't* come back with — with blood all over you? And a key to this house in your pocket? And a piece of the — of the shiny stuff off that snuff-box sticking to your dressing robe? *That's not true, is it?*"

A paralysis held the kindly atmosphere of this drawing room. The big spaniel whined in its throat for more food. Helena Lawes slowly fumbled after a spectacle case; she took out a pair of rimless nose glasses, pinched them on, and stared through them. Her mouth remained half open.

"Really, Janice!" she said severely.

"What I'm saying," retorted Janice, "I got from the prefect of police himself. I did, too!" she insisted, as they started to speak.

Uncle Ben Phillips brushed crumbs off his lap. He absentmindedly and affectionately tweaked the ears of the spaniel. He reached into his pocket after the inevitable pipe. His worried forehead and gentle, ice-blue eyes showed a nagging of wonder which he instantly and shamefacedly covered up.

"I was at the Donjon Hotel," explained Janice. "Having a drink."

"Janice, dear." Helena spoke mechanically. "I *wish* you wouldn't go to those —"

"I overheard Goron talking to a doctor, an awfully big shot in criminal psychology. He's English; I mean, the doctor is, not Goron; I've seen his picture

somewhere. Goron said that Eve came in that night
all over blood, with a piece of the snuff-box sticking
to her."

Still Janice looked away from everybody. Shock
was passing. Horror had come in instead.

"He says they've got two witnesses, Yvette and
Célestine, who saw her. The police have got her
negligée; there was blood on it. . . ."

Eve Neill was sitting back in her chair, rigidly.
She stared at Janice without seeing her. Eve wanted
to burst out laughing, and go on laughing, to drown
out the ominous and evil noises in her head.

Accusing *her* of murder! It should have been funny, if it hadn't taken her like a blow under the heart.
It *was* funny, in a way. But that incredible part about
a "piece of the snuff-box" sticking to her — the one
thing she could not understand in a whirl of ugly
absurdities — wasn't funny at all. It must be some
misunderstanding, or else malice was following her
to shut her into a corner and kill her. Of course, she
told herself, she needn't be afraid of the police. That
last monstrosity, the accusation of killing poor old
Papa Lawes, could easily be disproved. She could
always explain about Ned Atwood, and he would
confirm her.

She could prove she hadn't murdered anybody.
But to explain about Ned. . . .

"This is the most ridiculous thing I ever heard of!" she cried. "Please, at least, let me get my breath!"

"It *isn't* true, is it?" Janice was persisting.

Eve made a fierce gesture.

"No, of course it isn't true!" said Eve. "That is —"

A desperate hesitation struck at her. Her voice wavered, and the wavering was as palpable, as suggestive, as a comment.

"No, of course not," said Uncle Ben firmly. He cleared his throat.

"No, of course not!" echoed Helena.

"Then why," persisted Janice, "did you say, 'that is?' "

"I — I don't understand."

"You started off all right," Janice said. "Then you sort of chewed at your lip, and your eyes got all funny, and you qualified it by 'that is' as though there'd really been something else after all."

(Oh, God, what am I going to *say?*)

"None of it's true, is it?" asked Janice feverishly. "It can't be partly true and partly untrue, now can it?"

"There is certainly," observed Uncle Ben, clearing his throat again and speaking with some reluctance, "something in what the girl says."

Three pairs of eyes, kindly eyes, eyes which no doubt meant well towards her, were fastened on

Eve. For a second she had difficulty in getting her breath.

If realization came slowly, it came with none the less certainty. All these things were lies and misunderstandings. Or worse, like that "bit off the snuff-box" which danced in her mind with such tantalizing and terrifying repetition. But some of these things were facts. The police could prove them. It was no earthly good denying them.

"Tell me," Eve said, trying to reach firm ground. "Do you honestly think that I, of all people, would ever want to ... well, *hurt* ... him, of all people?"

"No, dear, of course not," Helena assured her. The near-sighted eyes grew pleading. "Just tell us there's no truth in this. That's all we want to know."

"Eve," Janice said quietly, "what kind of a life were you leading before you met Toby?"

It was the first personal question of any kind which had ever been asked her in this house.

"Now, really, Janice!" Helena protested, and grew more fussed than ever.

Janice paid no attention. Janice came over softly and sat down in a low upholstered chair facing Eve. The fair, almost transparent skin which so often accompanies red hair can, in moments of emotion, assume an unpleasantly bluish tinge. Janice's large brown eyes were fixed on Eve. Their expression was a mixture of admiration and repulsion.

"Don't think I'm blaming you for it!" she said, with the off-handed grandeur of twenty-three. "I rather admire you for it, really. I always have. I'm only talking about it now because the prefect of police was talking about it. I mean, the reason why you might have wanted to hurt Daddy. I don't say you did, mind! I don't even think you did. That is, necessarily. Only. . ."

Uncle Ben coughed.

"I hope we're all broad-minded," said Helena. "That is, all except Toby and perhaps poor Maurice — a bit. But, really, Janice!"

Janice ignored this.

"You were married to that Atwood man, weren't you?"

"Yes," said Eve. "Of course I was."

"He's back in La Bandelette, you know."

Eve moistened her lips.

"Is he?"

"Yes. A week ago today he was in the back bar of the Donjon, talking. Among other things, including the fact that you were still in love with him, he said he was going to get you back even if he had to tell our family everything about you."

Eve sat motionless. Her heart seemed briefly to

stop, and then to assume an enormous, pounding rhythm. The sheer injustices of this kept her dumb.

Janice craned her neck round.

"Do you remember," she went on, "the afternoon of the — the night Daddy died?"

Helena's eyes squeezed up.

"How he came back here," Janice pursued, "looking frightfully queer and quiet, and in a temper? And how he refused to go to the theatre with us? But wouldn't say why? And only the art dealer's calling up about the snuff-box put him in a good temper afterwards? Also, he said something to Toby before we went to the theatre? And Toby's been acting queerly ever since?"

"Well?" prompted Uncle Ben, carefully examining the bowl of a pipe.

"Nonsense," said Helena. But the tears started to her eyes at mention of that night, and her round face lost all its laughter lines and some of its color. "Toby was only behaving so stuffily that night because *Mrs. Warren's Profession* is a play about — well, about prostitution."

Eve sat up straight.

"Daddy's favorite afternoon walk," said Janice, "was in the Zoological Gardens at the back of the Donjon Hotel. Suppose this Mr. Atwood went after him, and told him something about. . ."

Janice did not complete the sentence. She nodded her head towards Eve without looking round.

"Then Daddy came home in that queer white way. He said something to Toby. Toby wouldn't believe him. Just suppose this, that's all! But Toby, you remember, couldn't sleep that night. He called Eve up at one o'clock in the morning. Suppose he told her what Daddy had said? Then suppose Eve came over here to fight it out with Daddy, and. . ."

"Just one moment, please," Eve said very quietly.

She allowed her quickened breathing to slow down before she spoke again.

"What have you really been thinking about me, all this time?" she asked.

"Nothing, dear! Nothing!" cried Helena, fumbling at her noseglasses, and taking them off. "There's never been anybody like you! Oh, dear, I never can find a handkerchief when I want one! Only, when Janice starts talking about blood and heaven knows what other things, and you don't come straight out and deny it. . ."

"Yes," said Uncle Ben.

"But that's not the only thing," persisted Eve. "I honestly want to know. What are all these cross currents and hints, and all the things you've never said until now? Are you intimating that 'Mrs. War-

ren's Profession' ought to be 'Mrs. Neill's Profession?'
Is that it?"

Helena was shocked.

"No, dear. Good heavens, no!"

"Then what is it? I know what people say about
me, or at least what they used to say. It isn't true. But,
if I hear it very much longer, I'm jolly well going to
make it true!"

"What about murder, though?" Janice asked
quietly.

Janice had the simplicity of a child. She was no
longer the bouncing, swaggering girl who aped a
dry sophistication and turned up her nose at the
amusements of those of her own age. She sat in the
low chair with her arms cradled round her knees.
The shiny-looking lids winked over the brown eyes.
Her lips were unsteady.

"You see," she explained, "it's just because we did
idealize you so much that. . ."

Again her gesture completed the sentence. Eve,
whose heart went out to these people, found herself
in a still more difficult position.

"Are you still in love with Mr. Atwood?" Janice
demanded.

"No!"

"And have you been playing the hypocrite all
this week? Is there something you haven't told us?"

"No. That is —"

"I thought," muttered Uncle Ben, "she'd been looking a bit peaky. But then we all have." He had taken out a clasp knife and was scraping the inside of the pipe bowl. Now his heavy, harassed face lifted. He looked at Helena. "Do you remember, dolly?"

"Remember what?" said Helena.

"I was working on the car. All I did was reach out and touch her with my glove, those brown leather work gloves, and she almost fainted. It wasn't a very clean glove, I admit."

Eve put up her hands to her eyes.

"Nobody believes the stories about you," Helena was saying gently. "But this other thing is different." She wheezed a little. "You still haven't answered Janice's question. Were you out of the house that night?"

"Yes," said Eve.

"And *was* there blood on you?"

"Yes. A little."

Now in the big drawing room, where the afterglow of sunset still lingered against the windows, there was no sound except the snuffling of the spaniel, who scratched the hardwood floor and lay down drowsily with his ears flopping between his paws. Even the small, sharp noise of Uncle Ben's knife scraping the pipe bowl had stopped. Three persons in sombre clothes, the two women in black and the man in dark gray, stared back at Eve with varying degrees of shock or incredulity.

"Don't look at me like that!" Eve almost screamed. "It isn't true. I hadn't anything to do with killing him. I was fond of him. It's nothing but a misunderstanding; only it's a frightful kind of misunderstanding that I can't seem to get out of."

Janice was white to the lips. "Did you come over here that night?"

"No. I swear I didn't!"

"Then why was there a k-key to this house in the pocket of your pajamas?"

"It wasn't a key to this house. It was a key to my house. It hadn't anything to *do* with your house! I wanted to tell you what really happened that night. I've been wanting to tell you ever since then. Only I didn't dare tell you."

"Oh?" said Helena. "Why couldn't you tell us?"

Even before she spoke, Eve realized the twisted and not altogether mirthful irony of what she must say. But many people would consider it funny. If there were ironic deities presiding over her destiny, they must be splitting their sides now. You could hear brazen laughter clanging at every word.

"I didn't dare tell you," she replied, "because Ned Atwood was in my bedroom."

VIII

M. ARISTIDE GORON and Dr. Dermot Kinross walked into the rue des Anges at a faster pace than the tubby prefect liked.

"This is luck!" he was fuming. "This is the luck of the devil! The little Miss Janice, no doubt, will have gone straight to Madame Neill with her story."

"I consider it very likely," agreed Dermot.

The prefect of police wore a bowler hat which accentuated his bulbousness, and carried a malacca stick. He stumped along with spatted feet beside Dermot's long stride, and growled in his throat.

"If you are to do me the favor of speaking to Madame Neill, and giving me your candid impression, it had better be done now. The examining magistrate will be furious. I telephoned to him, but he was out. When he hears, I know what he will do. He will send the salad basket immediately, and Madame Neill will sleep tonight in the violin."

Dermot blinked at him.

"Salad basket? Violin?"

"Ah! I forgot! The salad basket is . . ." M. Goron

groped for words. He made elaborate illustrative gestures, not very clearly.

"Black Maria?" hazarded Dermot.

"That's it! That's it! I have heard the term. And this violin is what you call in English the clink or show-kee."

"Chokey. Hard 'ch' sound."

"I make a note of it," said M. Goron, producing his microscopic memorandum book. "But I flatter myself that I speak English rather well, eh? Always I speak it to the Lawes family."

"You speak English very well. Only I entreat you not to say 'intercourse' when you mean 'interview.'"

M. Goron inclined his head. "It is not the same thing?"

"It is not at all the same thing. But. . ."

Dermot stopped on the pavement. He glanced round that quiet street, swept and domestic and provincial in the evening light. A few chestnut trees showed their leaves over gray garden walls.

Not many of his colleagues in London would have recognized Dr. Kinross then. It was partly the effect of holiday clothes, a baggy sports suit and comfortably disreputable hat. Since his stay in La Bandelette he looked less tired, less powerfully geared to a work that never let him go. There was more of a twinkle in his eye and more animation in the dark face which only in certain lights showed any trace of plastic surgery. That is, there had been this loosening or relaxing until he had heard M. Goron's story of the murder told in detail.

Dermot frowned.

"Which," he asked, "is Madame Neill's house?"

"We are standing beside it." M. Goron reached out his malacca stick and touched the high gray wall on his left. "And, of course, the house directly across the road is the Villa Bonheur."

Dermot turned to look.

Square and sedate and white-faced was the Villa Bonheur, with a grimy, red tiled roof. Its own wall cut off your view of the ground floor windows. On the floor above were six windows, two to a room. It was at the center two — the only full-length windows on that floor, which had a filigree-railed balcony outside them — that Dermot and M. Goron looked. The gray painted steel shutters were uncompromisingly closed.

"It would interest me very much," Dermot said, "to see the inside of that study."

"My dear doctor! Nothing is easier." M. Goron gestured over his shoulder, towards Eve's house. His agitation had increased. "But if we are to see Madame Neill now?"

Dermot paid no attention.

"Was it Sir Maurice's habit," he asked, "to sit up there in the evenings with the curtains drawn back from the windows?"

"I believe so. The weather was very hot."

"Then surely the murderer ran a devil of a risk?"

"Of what?"

"Of being seen," — Dermot pointed, — "from an upper window of any of these other houses on this side of the street."

"No, I do not think so."

"Why not?"

M. Goron shrugged his well-tailored shoulders.

"The season in our fine city," he said, "is nearly over. Few of these villas are now occupied. You notice how deserted the whole street seems?"

"Well?"

"Certainly the villa on each side of Madame Neill's house is vacant. Rest assured, we made inquiries until we were blue in the face. The only person who might possibly have seen something was Madame Neill herself. But, even if by any remote chance Madame Neill were *not* the assassin, still she would be unable to help us. It appears that she has what you would call a mania for keeping the curtains closed on her own windows."

Dermot pulled the brim of his hat down on his forehead.

"My friend," he said, "I don't like your evidence."

"Oho?"

"For instance, the motive assigned to Madame Neill is rubbish. Let me show you."

But he got no further. M. Goron, gripped by a profound interest, had peered left and right to make sure they were not overheard. Catching sight of a figure striding towards them along the pavement from the direction of the Boulevard du Casino, M. Goron seized his companion's arm. He impelled Dermot through the gateway in the wall round Eve's villa, and closed the gate afterwards.

"Monsieur," he hissed, "there is M. Horatio Lawes himself, coming with a purposeful walk and doubt-less intent on seeing Madame Neill too. If we are to do any good with her, we must get there first."

"But —"

"I beg of you, don't stop to look at M. Lawes! He is, heaven knows, ordinary enough. Forward, and ring at the door."

It was unnecessary to ring at the door. They had hardly reached the first of the two stone steps leading up to it, when the door was abruptly opened in their faces.

Their presence, evidently, was an equal surprise to the persons inside. A kind of squeal came from the semi-dark interior. Two women stood on the threshold, one with her hand on the knob of the door.

The first of the two women, Dermot thought, must obviously be Yvette Latour. She was a broad, heavy woman, strongly featured and dark-haired, yet so self-effacing that she seemed to blend with the interior of the hall. In her face, surprise was succeeded by a flash of malicious satisfaction which kindled the little black eyes and then dwindled to stolidity. But it was the presence of the other woman, a girl in her twenties, which made M. Goron's eyebrows rise nearly to the hair line.

"*Tiens?*" he intoned, sweeping off his hat and letting his voice rise to a hollow register. "*Tiens, tiens, tiens?*"

"I beg monsieur's pardon," intoned Yvette.

"Not at all, not at all!"

"This is my sister, monsieur," said Yvette smoothly. "She was just leaving."

"*A'voir*, dearie," said the girl.

"*A'voir*, baby," replied Yvette, with a real warmth of affection. "Be good. My regards to our mama."

And the girl came sweeping out.

It was easy to see the family likeness. But there all resemblance to Yvette ended.

This girl was slim, she was smartly dressed in very good taste, she was demure, she was — in that one word — chic. Her large dark eyes regarded them with that glance of frank appraisal, combined with a pouting laugh of the mouth and a joyous sense of well-being, which only a Frenchwoman can get away with. She seemed to twinkle with impudence at the same time that she demurely eluded you. The perfume she wore (there was perhaps a little too much of it) spread round her as she came floating down the two steps.

"Mademoiselle Prue," observed M. Goron, with formal gallantry.

"Monsieur," said the girl respectfully. She ducked him a kind of curtsy. Then she was gone down the path.

"We are looking," the prefect said to Yvette, "for Madame Neill."

"Then I regret, M. Goron, that you will have to go opposite. Madame Neill is taking tea with the Lawes family."

"I thank you, mademoiselle."

"Not at all, monsieur!"

Yvette kept her expression of stolid politeness. But, just before the door closed, there flashed across her face an expression Dermot was unable to read. It might have been mockery. M. Goron stood staring at the closed door, tapping the head of his stick against his teeth, before he replaced his hat.

"*Tiens?*" he muttered. "My friend, I have a feeling that —"

"Yes?"

"That this little episode ought to mean something. But I don't know what."

"I have the same feeling," Dermot admitted.

"Those two were plotting something. I could smell it. Such are the instincts we develop. But beyond that I should not care to venture a guess."

"You know the girl?"

"Mademoiselle Prue? Oh, yes."

"Is she. . ."

"Respectable, were you going to say?" M. Goron suddenly chuckled. "Tiens, that is the first question you English always ask!" But he considered the question with some care, his head on one side. "Yes, so far as I know she is as respectable as need be. She owns a flower shop in the rue de la Harpe. Not far, by the way, from the antique shop of my friend M. Veille."

"That's the dealer who sold the snuff-box to Sir Maurice Lawes?"

"Yes. But was not paid for it." Again the prefect hesitated. "But this," he complained, making a tolerably hideous face, "achieves us nothing. We cannot stop to debate the evidence of why Mademoiselle Prue should call on her sister, or even why the devil she shouldn't. We came here to see Madame Neill. It will be much simpler if we go across the street and discover what Madame Neill has to say herself."

They found out soon enough.

The front garden of the Villa Bonheur was a trim grass plot behind a brick wall. The front door was closed. But the long windows immediately to the right of it stood wide open. At past six o'clock in the evening, shadows were gathering across that garden; the drawing room beyond showed dusky. But it was as charged with emotion as though with electricity. As M. Goron pushed open the gate, they heard a voice issuing from the drawing room. It was a young girl's voice, speaking in English. Dermot imagined Janice Lawes's vibrant personality as clearly as though he could see her.

"Go on!" the voice urged.

"I —— I can't," said another woman's voice after a pause.

"Don't look like that! And don't stop," begged Janice, "just because Toby's come barging in!"

"Look here," interposed a heavy male voice, speaking with evident bewilderment, "what *is* all this?"

"Toby, my dear, I've been trying to tell you!"

"I've had a hard day at the office. None of you women ever seem to appreciate that. And the poor old governor didn't leave his affairs in any too good shape. I'm not in the mood for games."

"Games?" echoed Janice.

"Yes, games! Let a fellow alone, can't you?"

"On the night Daddy was killed," said Janice, "Eve was out of her house and came back all covered with blood. She was carrying a key to our front door. There was a chip of agate from the snuff-box stuck in the lace of her dressing robe."

Beckoning to his companion, M. Goron stepped noiselessly across the firm grass and peered in at the nearer window.

The long drawing room was much cluttered with furniture. Its floor glimmered, a pale lake that seemed lighter than the sky. This was a comfortable room, a lived-in room of many ashtrays and possessions put down to be picked up again. A golden-brown spaniel slumbered by the tea wagon. The easy-chairs upholstered in some rough tan material, the white marble mantelpiece, the bowl of blue-and-flame asters on a side table, made faint color against dusk. But the sombrely dressed people here seemed little more than shadows, except for the living entity of their faces.

From M. Goron's descriptions, it was easy for Dermot to pick out Helena Lawes, and Benjamin Phillips sitting by the tea wagon with an empty pipe

in his mouth. Janice sat in a low chair with her back
to the windows.

Eve Neill could not be seen at all, since Toby
Lawes was in the way. Toby, wearing a sober gray
suit with a correct black mourning band round the
sleeve, stood by the fireplace. His face bore a slightly
foolish expression, and one hand was raised as though
to shade his eyes.

He stared uncomprehendingly from Janice to his
mother, and back again. Even his small mustache
seemed eloquent. Then his voice went high.

"For God's sake, what are you talking about?"

"Of course, Toby," Helena said hesitantly,
"there's an explanation."

"Explanation?"

"Yes. It was all because of Mr. Atwood, Eve's
husband."

"Oh?" said Toby.

Even in the midst of his evident shock at what
must have been incomprehensible words, Toby's eyebrows went up. There was a slight pause before that
monosyllable came floating out on the evening air. It
was repressed and self-contained. Yet to an attentive
ear it was full of meaning, poisoned with jealousy.

"I say, mother." Toby moistened his lips. "You
might remember that the fellow isn't married to Eve
any longer."

"But *he* wouldn't remember it, Eve says," put in Janice. "He came back to La Bandelette."

"Yes. I'd heard he was back." Toby spoke mechanically. Then he took away the hand that shaded his eyes; and he made what was, for him, an almost wild gesture. "What I want to know is, what is all this about . . . about. . . ."

"Mr. Atwood," replied Janice, "broke into Eve's house on the night Daddy died."

"Broke into it?"

"That is, he had a key he'd kept from other days when he lived there. He came upstairs after she was undressed."

Toby stood rigid.

So far as it could be read in the gloom, his expression remained a blank. He took one step backwards, bumping into the mantelpiece and groping before he recovered himself. He started to glance round towards Eve, but apparently thought better of it.

"Go on," he said huskily.

"But it's not *my* story," said Janice. "Ask Eve herself. She'll tell you. Eve, you've got to go on! Don't let Toby worry you! Just tell us about it as though Toby weren't here at all."

M. Aristide Goron, prefect of police of La Bandelette, uttered a low growl deep in his throat. He drew a deep breath. His round, bland face smoothed itself out into affable lines. He threw back his shoulders, and removed his hat. Stepping forward briskly, so that his footfalls clacked on the polished hardwood, he swept into the drawing room.

"And as though you did not find me here either, Madame Neill," he said.

IX

Ten minutes later M. Goron was sitting in a chair and leaning forward with catlike attention, prompting her. He had begun the examination, with a flourish, in English. Then he had got excited, tangled himself up in long incomprehensible sentences, and finally flowed straight into French.

"Yes, madame?" he queried, with the effect of prodding her gently with one finger. "And then?"

"What else can I *say*?" cried Eve.

"M. Atwood," said the prefect, "crept upstairs with this key. Good! He attempted to," — M. Goron cleared his throat, — "overcome you. Eh?"

"Yes."

"This, of course, was against your will?"

"Of course!"

"Understood!" M. Goron soothed her. "And then, madame?"

"I begged him please to be decent and go away and not make a scene, because Sir Maurice Lawes was sitting across here in the room opposite."

"And then?"

"He started to pull back the curtains, to see whether Sir Maurice was still sitting up in the study. I turned out the light —"

"You turned out the light?"

"Yes, certainly!"

M. Goron frowned. "Forgive my obtuseness, madame. But surely that was an extraordinary way of discouraging M. Atwood's attentions?"

"I tell you, I didn't want Sir Maurice to *know!*"

M. Goron pondered this.

"Then madame admits," he suggested, "that it was the fear of discovery which caused madame to be . . . shall we say . . . obdurate?"

"No, no, no!"

Twilight was deepening in the long drawing room. The various members of the Lawes family sat or stood like wax figures. Their faces held little expression, or at least little expression that could be read. Toby remained by the fireplace, now turned towards it and holding out his hands automatically towards a fire which did not exist.

The prefect of police did not bully or threaten. His expression remained worried. M. Goron, a man and a Frenchman, was merely trying in all honesty to understand a situation which baffled him.

"You feared this man Atwood?"

"Yes, very much."

"Yet you did not attempt to call out to Sir Maurice, even though he was within sight and hearing?"

"I tell you, I *couldn't!*"

"Par example, what was Sir Maurice doing then?"

"He was sitting," answered Eve, recalling a scene which by now had been impressed on her mind with unbearable vividness, "he was sitting at his desk, holding up a magnifying glass to look at something. There was —"

"Yes, madame?"

She had intended to add, "There was somebody with him." But, in front of the Lawes family, and considering what this might imply, it stuck in her throat. Again her imagination saw the old man's lips moving, the magnifying glass, and the shadow hovering behind.

"There was the snuff-box," she substituted weakly. "He was looking at it."

"At what time was this, madame?"

"I — I don't remember!"

"And then?"

"Ned came over towards me. I fought him off. I begged him not to wake the servants." Eve was pouring out the truth, every word of it; yet, at that last sentence, the faces of her auditors altered slightly. "Don't you see? I didn't want the servants to learn about it either. Then the telephone rang."

"Ah!" said M. Goron with satisfaction. "In that case, it should be easy to establish the time." He craned round. "I think it was at just one o'clock, M. Lawes, that you telephoned to madame?"

Toby nodded. But he was paying no attention to this. He spoke casually to Eve.

"Then all the time you were speaking to me," Toby said, "that fellow was actually in your room?"

"I'm sorry, dear! I tried to keep it from you!"

"Yes," agreed Janice, sitting motionless in the low chair. "You did."

"Standing beside you," muttered Toby. "Sitting beside you. Maybe even . . ." He made a gesture. "You sounded so calm, too. As though it didn't matter a damn. As though you'd just waked up in the middle of the night, and couldn't think of a thing but me."

"Continue, if you please," interrupted M. Goron.

"After that," said Eve, "I ordered him out. Still he wouldn't go. He said he wasn't going to allow me to make a mistake."

"Meaning what, madame?"

"He thought I oughtn't to marry Toby. And he thought he could make people think things about me, things that weren't true, if he leaned out of the window and shouted across to Sir Maurice that he was in my bedroom. Ned goes completely mad when he gets an idea like that. He went to the window. I ran after him. But, when we looked out . . ."

Eve turned up the palms of her hands. To Dermot Kinross, to Aristide Goron, to anyone with a sensitiveness to atmospheres, the ensuing pause seemed definitely sinister.

It was full of small noises. Helena Lawes, her hand at her breast, gave a tiny cough. Benjamin Phillips, who had been carefully filling his pipe, now struck a match for it; the little snap and rasp was like a comment before the flame curled up. Janice remained motionless, her wide and innocent brown eyes seeming slowly to realize what this might mean. But it was Toby who spoke.

"You looked out of the window?" he demanded.

Eve nodded violently.

"*When?*"

"Just after . . ."

She needed to say no more than that. Little whispering voices struck across at her. It was as though those low voices dared not speak loudly, lest they spring an ambush or raise ghosts.

"You didn't see —?" began Helena.

"Anybody?" prompted Janice.

"Anything?" mumbled Uncle Ben.

Sitting quietly in a corner where nobody noticed him, his chin in his fist and his eyes never leaving

Eve Neill, Dermot fixed his mind with a painful intensity on the meaning that might underlie her halting, unconvincing story.

The analytical side of his mind registered: Strong thyroid type. Imaginative. Easily suggestible. Good-natured and generous, perhaps too much so for her own good. Intensely loyal to any person who has shown her a kindness. Yes: this woman might very well commit murder, if sufficiently impelled. And Dermot found this a disturbing thought, which struck and stabbed through the tough hide he had been building round his own emotions for twenty years.

He watched her as she sat in the big tan-upholstered easy-chair. He watched her fingers clenching and uncurling on the arms of it. He watched the delicate face, lips pinched together, and the small nerve that throbbed in her neck. A little wrinkle in her forehead seemed to poise a desperate question. He watched the gray eyes move from Toby to Janice, then from Janice to Helena and Uncle Ben, and back to Toby again.

And Dermot thought: this woman is going to tell a lie.

"No!" cried Eve; and her body stiffened as though she had made a decision. "We didn't see anybody. Or anything."

"*We*," said Toby, and struck his hand on the top of the mantelpiece. " 'We' didn't see anything!"

M. Goron silenced him with a look.

"Yet it appears," he pursued, with a dangerous blandness, "that madame witnessed something. Was Sir Maurice dead?"

"Yes!"

"You could see him clearly?"

"Yes!"

"Then how does madame know," said the prefect suavely, "that it was 'just after' he had been killed?"

"I don't, of course." Eve spoke after a slight pause. The gray eyes looked straight back at M. Goron; her breast rose and fell slowly. "I mean, I only assume it must have been."

"Continue, please," breathed M. Goron, and flicked his fingers in the air.

"Poor Helena came in and began screaming. This time I ordered Ned out, and I meant it."

"Oh? Madame had not meant it before?"

"I had! I tell you I had! Only this time, I mean, it was so serious that he knew he had to go. Before he went, I got back that key from him and put it in the pocket of my pajamas. On his way down, he . . ." Here she appeared to realize the grotesqueness, almost the absurdity, of what she had to tell.

"On the way down, he slipped on the stairs and hurt his nose."

"His *nose?*" repeated M. Goron.

"Yes. It bled. I touched him, and that was how I got some blood on my hand and splashed on my clothes. This blood that you've been fussing over so much was really Ned Atwood's blood."

"Indeed, madame?"

"You don't have to ask me! Ask Ned! He may not be all he should be, but at least he'll be decent enough to confirm every word I say when you put me in a position like this."

"Will he, madame?"

Again Eve nodded violently. She cast a quick glance of entreaty and appeal at the persons who stood round her. This woman was beginning to cloud Dermot Kinross's judgment. It was uncanny and damnable. He had never before felt quite like this in his life. Yet the coldly reasoning part of his brain told him that Eve — except at the one point where she had hesitated — was speaking the truth.

"Concerning M. Atwood," the prefect went on. "You tell me that he 'slipped on the stairs and hurt his nose.' Was there no other injury?"

"No other injury? I don't understand?"

"He did not hurt — for example — his head?"

Eve frowned. "I can't say. He might very well

have done. That is a high, steep staircase, and he took a most terrible tumble. I couldn't see what happened in the dark. But the blood at least was from his nose."

M. Goron smiled in a faint and far-away manner, like one who has expected this.

"Continue, dear madame!"

"I let him out by the back door. . . ."

"Why the back door?"

"Because the street outside was full of policemen. He went away. And that was when it happened. The back door of my house has a spring lock. While I was standing there, the wind blew the door shut and I was locked out."

After a slight pause, during which the members of the Lawes family slowly directed curious glances at each other, Helena spoke on a note of gentle remonstrance. Helena wheezed a little.

"Surely, my dear, you must be mistaken?" she demanded. "The *wind* blew your door shut? Don't you remember?"

"There wasn't a breath of wind that whole night," interposed Janice. "We talked about it while we were at the theatre."

"I —— I know."

"Then, my dear!" protested Helena.

"I mean, I thought of that too. It only occurred to me afterwards, when I was trying to think of some possible explanation, that somebody might have — well, might have deliberately pushed it shut."

"Oho?" said M. Goron. "Who?"

"Yvette. My maid." Eve clenched her hands and almost writhed in the chair. "Why does she detest me so much?"

M. Goron's eyebrows travelled still higher.

"Let me understand you, madame. You are accusing Yvette Latour of deliberately shutting the door from inside and locking you out?"

"I swear to all of you that I don't know what I'm suggesting! I'm trying as hard as I can to find out what might have happened."

"And so are we, madame. Continue this interesting recital. You are in the back garden. . . ?"

"Don't you see? I was locked out! I couldn't get in."

"Couldn't get in? Sacred name! Madame had only to knock at the door or ring at the bell, surely?"

"Which would have roused the servants, and that's what I didn't want. I couldn't endure the idea of waking up Yvette. . . ."

"Who had just, it appears, woken herself up and for some reason locked madame out. I beg of you," added M. Goron, making hollow-sounding noises of sympathy, "that you will not upset yourself. I do not seek to trap or trick madame. I only try to establish . . . shall we say? . . . the truth as she tells it."

"But that's all there is!"

"All?"

"I remembered that I had a key to the front door in the pocket of my pajamas. I slipped round to the front, and got in. That's how I came to lose my sash; I can't even remember yet where I lost it, but I noticed it was gone when I was — well, washing myself."

"Ah!"

"I suppose you must have found it, too?"

"Yes, madame. Forgive me for directing attention to it; but there is one small matter which this story does not explain. I refer to the chip of agate found entangled in the lace of madame's dressing gown."

Eve spoke quietly.

"I don't know anything about it. You must please believe me when I say that." She pressed her hands over her eyes, and took them away again. She spoke with a passionate sincerity which must have impressed her listeners. "This is the first time I've heard anything about it! I can almost swear it wasn't there when I came back to the house. Because, as I told you, I took off the negligée to wash. I can only think that somebody must have put it there afterwards."

"Put it there," observed M. Goron: a statement rather than a question.

Eve started to laugh. She looked incredulously from one face to another.

"But you surely can't be thinking of me as a *murderer?*"

"In candor, madame, this fantastic idea has been suggested."

"But I can . . . don't you see? I can *prove* every word I say is true!"

"How, madame?" inquired the prefect, and began to tap his well-manicured fingers on the little table beside his chair.

Eve appealed to the others.

"I'm sorry. I didn't tell you about it before, because I didn't want to tell you about Ned being in my room."

"That's understandable enough," observed Janice in a colorless voice.

"But this," — Eve spread out her hands, — "*this* is so utterly ridiculous that I can't even think what to say to it. It's like being waked up in the middle of the night and accused of killing somebody you never even heard of. I should be frightened to death, if I didn't know I could prove what I say."

"I must distress madame by repeating my question," said M. Goron. "How is this to be proved?"

"By Ned Atwood, of course!"

"Ah," said the prefect of police.

His movements were very deliberate. He lifted the lapel of his coat to sniff at the white rose in the buttonhole. His eyes were fixed at a neutral point on the floor. He made a slight gesture. But his face betrayed nothing except a heavy frown.

"Tell me, madame. You have had all week, I believe, to consider this story of yours?"

"I haven't considered anything! This is the first time I've heard of all these things. I'm telling you the truth!"

M. Goron lifted his eyes.

"Has madame, perhaps, seen M. Atwood at any time during this week?"

"No, certainly not!"

"Are you still in love with him, Eve?" Janice asked in a low voice. "*Are* you still in love with him?"

"No, dear, of course not," Helena interposed soothingly.

"Thank you very much," said Eve. She looked at Toby. "Do I have to tell you that? I loathe and detest him. I never despised anybody so much in my life. I never want to set eyes on him again."

"It is unlikely, I think," observed M. Goron softly, "that madame ever will see him again."

They all swung round. M. Goron, who had again fallen to a study of the floor, raised his eyes once more.

"Surely madame knows that M. Atwood is in no condition to verify her story, even if he wished to do so?" M. Goron's voice sharpened. "Surely madame knows that M. Atwood has been lying at the Donjon Hotel, suffering from concussion of the brain?"

It was perhaps ten seconds before Eve rose to her feet, pushing herself up out of the deep chair. She stared back at the prefect. She was wearing, Dermot noticed for the first time, a gray silk blouse and black skirt. It contrasted with her pink-and-white complexion, with the wide-set gray eyes. But Dermot — who seemed to himself to be conscious of every nerve in her body and every thought in her head — felt a new emotion.

Hitherto, he guessed, these accusations had been no more than a poor, ironic joke. Now, suddenly, she saw it differently. She saw where the whole thing might lead. It couldn't be leading there, and yet it was. She saw the imminence of danger, deadly danger, flowing from every bland gesture of the prefect and every temperate word he spoke.

"Concussion of . . ." she began.

M. Goron nodded.

"A week ago, at half-past one in the morning," he continued, "M. Atwood walked into the foyer of the Donjon. In the elevator, going up to his room, he collapsed."

Eve pressed her hands to her temples.

"But that was when he left me! It was dark. I couldn't see. He must have hit his head when he . . ." After a pause she added: "Poor old Ned!"

Toby Lawes struck his fist on top of the mantelpiece.

A faintly satiric smile marred the politeness of M. Goron's face.

"Unfortunately," he pursued, "M. Atwood retained consciousness long enough to explain that he had been knocked over by a car in the street, and struck his head against the curbstone. That was his final word."

Here M. Goron drew one finger across in the air, as though delicately underlining a point.

"You understand, M. Atwood will probably not testify to anything now. He is not expected to recover."

X

M. Goron looked doubtful.

"I should not perhaps have told you that," he added. "Yes. I have been indiscreet. It is not customary to be so frank with the accused before their arrest. . . ."

"Arrest?" screamed Eve.

"I must warn you to expect it, madame."

Emotion had reached too high a pitch. The others could confine themselves to speaking French no longer.

"They can't do that," wheezed Helena, with tears in her eyes. Her lower lip was thrust out defiantly. "Not to a British subject, they can't. Poor Maurice was one of the Consul's greatest friends. All the same, Eve —"

"It does take a bit of explaining," Janice cried in bewilderment. "The chip off that snuff-box, I mean. And why you didn't call out for help, if you were really afraid of this Mr. Atwood. That's what *I* should have done."

Toby kicked moodily at the fender.

"What beats me," he muttered, "is that the fellow was actually in the room when I telephoned."

Uncle Ben said nothing. He was seldom inclined to say anything. Uncle Ben was the man who worked with his hands, who could repair a car or whittle a toy boat or paper a wall against any professional. He remained by the tea wagon, smoking his pipe. Occasionally he would give Eve the ghost of an encouraging smile, but his mild eye looked worried and he continued to shake his head.

"With regard," M. Goron continued in English, "to this question of restraining Mrs. Neill under arrest . . ."

"One moment," said Dermot.

All were startled when he spoke.

They had never seen, or at least never noticed him, where he sat in the darkish corner by the piano. Now Eve's eyes rested on him fully. For a second he felt a twinge of that old panic and self-consciousness he had once known when he thought he must go through life without half a face. It was a relic of evil days. It was a relic of days when he had realized that mental suffering is the worst suffering on this earth, and had chosen his profession accordingly.

M. Goron jumped up.

"Ah, my God!" the prefect said dramatically. "I am forgetting! My friend! I deeply apologize if I am impolite against you. But in this excitement . . ."

Here the prefect swept out his hand.

"I would wish to present my friend Dr. Kinross, from England. These are the peoples I have told you of. Milady Lawes. The brother, the daughter, the son. And Madame Neill. How do you do? You do well, I trust? Yes."

Toby Lawes froze.

"You're English?" he demanded.

"Yes," smiled Dermot. "I'm English. But please don't let it worry you."

"I thought you were one of Goron's people," said Toby, with a sense of grievance asserting itself. "Damn it all, we were *talking*." He glanced round. "I mean, pretty freely!"

"Oh, what does it matter?" said Janice.

"I'm very sorry," Dermot apologized. "My only excuse for intruding on you now is that —"

"I ask him," explained M. Goron. "In private he is a great doctor who practice in Vimpole Street. In public he has, to my knowledge, capture three big criminals. Once because a coat is buttoned wrong and once because he notices the way a person speak. Things of the mind, you see. So I ask him here —"

Dermot looked straight at Eve.

"Because my friend M. Goron," he said, "has some

doubt about the value of the evidence against Mrs. Neill."

"My friend!" cried the prefect, with angry reproachfulness.

"Isn't that so?"

"It is not necessarily so," answered M. Goron, in a highly sinister tone, "any longer."

"But my real reason for coming, and hoping I might be of service, is that I was once acquainted with your husband...."

"You knew Maurice?" cried Helena, as Dermot looked at her.

"Yes. In the old days, when I was doing prison work. He was very much interested in prison reform."

Helena wagged her head. Though bewildered at having an unexpected guest, she bounced up from her chair and tried to make him welcome. But the strain of the last week had evidently been too much. And, as usual when someone mentioned Maurice's name, there was another blink of tears in her eyes.

"Maurice," she said, "was more than just 'interested.' He used to study the people in those prisons, the convicts I mean, and know all about them. Even if they didn't know about *him*. Because, you see, he helped them and didn't want any credit for it." Her tone grew petulant. "Oh, dear, what am I saying?

It won't do any good to keep on thinking about that, will it?"

"Dr. Kinross," observed Janice in a small, clear voice.

"Yes?"

"Do they honestly mean all this talk about arresting Eve?"

"I hope not," Dermot said evenly.

"You hope not? Why?"

"Because in that case I should have to fight my old friend M. Goron from here to Llandudno."

"Since you've heard Eve's story, whether we like it or not, what do you think of it? Do you believe it?"

"Yes."

M. Goron's face was a study in polite rage. But he did not comment. The ease of Dermot's personality seemed to spread round them, drawing the wires from their nerves and making them feel easier in spite of themselves.

"It's not been easy to listen to this," observed Toby. "It's not been easy for us at all."

"Of course not. But has it occurred to you," said Dermot, "that it may have been rather embarrassing for Mrs. Neill too?"

"Having a stranger here," said Toby. "After all, damn it!"

"I'm sorry. I'll go."

Toby appeared to be struggling. "I didn't exactly say I wanted you to *go*," he growled. His good-humored face seemed tortured with doubt and discontent. "This is all too sudden! It's not the kind of thing to spring on a chap when he comes home from work. But you ought to know about these things, oughtn't you. Come to think of it, I know a chap who met you once. Do you think . . . that is. . . ?"

Dermot carefully refrained from looking at Eve.

She needed help. Sick with fright and uncertainty, she was standing beside the chair, her hands clasped together, trying to make Toby meet her eye. It needed no psychologist to tell that all she wanted was a word of reassurance from him. And she was not getting that word. An obscure anger crawled through Dermot Kinross as he saw it.

"Do you want me to speak frankly?" he asked.

Perhaps, in his heart of hearts, Toby didn't; but his gesture implied assent.

"Well," smiled Dermot, "I think you ought to make up your mind."

"Make up my mind?"

"Yes. Is Mrs. Neill guilty of infidelity, or is she guilty of murder? She can't be guilty of both, you know."

Toby opened his mouth, but shut it again.

And Dermot, moving his eyes from one to the

other of them, went on in the same heavy, patient tone as he addressed Toby.

"That's what you seem to be forgetting. In one breath you say you can't bear to think of Atwood being there when you were telephoning to her. In the next breath you shout for an explanation of how a chip from the snuff-box came to be tangled up in her robe. It seems rather rough on Mrs. Neill when you, her friends, try to have it both ways.

"You must make up your mind, Mr. Lawes. If she was over in this house murdering your father — from no reasonable motive that I can see — then Atwood certainly wasn't with her in her bedroom. The question of infidelity doesn't arise to shock you. And if Atwood *was* with her in the bedroom, then she certainly wasn't over here murdering your father." He paused. "Which one will you have, sir?"

The polished, ironic courtesy of his tone struck at Toby like a barb. It brought realization to them all.

"Doctor," said M. Goron, in a loud but steady voice, "I should like the favor of a word with you in private."

"Willingly."

"Madame would not mind —" M. Goron swung round to Helena, and spoke in a still louder voice, "— if Dr. Kinross and I went out into the foyer for a moment?"

He did not wait for a reply. Firmly taking hold of Dermot's arm, M. Goron marched him across the room like a schoolmaster. M. Goron opened the door to the hall, motioned Dermot to precede him, bowed briefly to those still in the room, and went out.

In the hall it was nearly dark. M. Goron touched a light switch, illuminating an arched, gray-tiled entrance with a stone staircase covered in red carpet. Breathing hard, the prefect of police hung up his hat and cane on the hat stand. He had followed the conversation in English with some difficulty; now, making sure that the door was closed, he addressed Dermot in angry French.

"My friend, you disappoint me."

"Many apologies."

"Furthermore, you betray me. I bring you here to be of some assistance. And, my God, what do you do? Will you tell me why you take this attitude?"

"The woman isn't guilty."

M. Goron took a few rapid little steps up and down the hall. He stopped only to give Dermot a very inscrutable, very Gallic look.

"Is that," he inquired politely, "the head or the heart which speaks?"

(Confound the fellow!)

"Come!" said M. Goron. "I had thought that you at least, the merchant of scientific fact — I think that was your own term? — would be impervious to the charms of Madame Neill. This woman is a public menace!"

"I tell you —!"

The other regarded him pityingly.

"Dear doctor, I am not a detective. No, no, no! But as for zizipompom, that is different. Any form of zizipompom I can detect at a distance of three kilometres and in the dark."

Dermot looked him in the eye. "On my word of honor," he retorted truthfully, "I don't believe she is guilty."

"This story of hers?"

"What's wrong with it?"

"My dear doctor! You ask me?"

"I do. This man Atwood falls on the stairs and cracks his head. Mrs. Neill's description was absolutely characteristic: I tell you that as a medical man. Bleeding from the nose, without injury to it, is one of the surest signs of concussion. Atwood gets up, thinking he is not seriously hurt; he walks to his hotel; and there he collapses. That's characteristic too."

At this word "characteristic," M. Goron seemed very thoughtful. But he did not pursue it.

"You say that, after M. Atwood's own statement . . . ?"

"Why not? He realizes that he is in a bad way. He

has the sense to realize that *nothing* must connect him with Mrs. Neill or the affair in the rue des Anges. How is he to know that she will be dragged into the murder as a principal? Who, in God's name, could have foreseen that? So he blurts out this story of being knocked over by a car."

M. Goron made a face.

"Of course," Dermot suggested, "you have compared specimens of Sir Maurice Lawes's blood with the blood found on this lady's sash and negligée?"

"Naturally. And both specimens, I may tell you, belong to the same blood-group."

"Which group?"

"Group Four."

Dermot raised his eyebrows. "That's not much good, is it? It's the commonest blood-group of all. Forty-one per cent of all Europeans belong to it. —Have you tested Atwood's blood too?"

"But naturally not! Why should we? This is the very first I have heard of madame's story!"

"Test it, then. If it comes from a different group, her story is automatically disproved."

"Ah!"

"But if, on the other hand, it also comes from Group Four, that's at least negative confirmation of what Mrs. Neill says. In any case, don't you think that in the interests of justice you ought to make the experiment before throwing that woman into prison and subjecting her to more refinements in the way of torture?"

M. Goron took another little run up and down the hall.

"Myself," he shouted, "I prefer to think that Madame Neill heard of M. Atwood's injury from the car, and used it to fit her story. Being very sure — mark you! — that the *also* love-sick M. Atwood will confirm whatever she says when he wakes up."

This, Dermot had to admit in his soul, was infernally plausible. He could have sworn he was right, but what if he were wrong? The disturbing effect of Eve Neill remained with him: he could imagine her presence now.

Yet he knew with fiery certainty that his judgment, his instincts, every weight of human logic as opposed to the logic of evidence, had not been mistaken. And, unless he fought back with every thrust and trick, they would have this woman in the dock for murder.

"Motive?" he suggested. "Have you even yet found a ghost of a motive?"

"To the devil with this motive!"

"Come, now! That's unworthy of you. Why did she kill Sir Maurice Lawes?"

"I told you this afternoon," returned M. Goron.

"It is theoretical, yes. But it marches. The afternoon before he is killed, Sir Maurice hears something of a monstrous nature against Madame Neill —"

"He hears what?"

"And how, in the name of a small green cabbage, should *I* know?"

"Then why suggest it?"

"Doctor, be silent and listen to me! The old man returns home, in that strange state they describe. He tells M. Horatio, this Tobee. Both are in a state of emotion. At one o'clock in the morning, M. Horatio telephones to Madame Neill and informs her of what they know. Madame Neill comes over, also in a state, to see Sir Maurice and debate this matter with him. . . ."

"Ah! So you also," interposed Dermot, "want to have it both ways?"

M. Goron blinked at him.

"Pardon?"

"You will notice," Dermot continued, "that this is what did NOT happen. There was no quarrel. There were no angry words. There was not even a confrontation. According to your own theory, the murderer walked in softly, stole up behind a deaf man, and struck him down without warning while he was still absorbed in his beloved snuff-box. Is this correct?"

M. Goron hesitated. "In effect —" he began.

"Well! You say Mrs. Neill did this. *Why* did she do it? Because Sir Maurice knew something about her which was also known to Toby Lawes, since Toby had just finished telling her about it over the telephone?"

"In a sense it is true...."

"Consider. I telephone to you in the middle of the night and I say, 'M. Goron, the examining magistrate has just told me you are a German spy and are going to be shot.' Do you immediately walk out and kill the examining magistrate, to prevent leakage of a secret already known to me? Similarly! If it were anything against Mrs. Neill's character, would she be likely to creep across the street and murder the father of her fiancé without so much as asking for a word of explanation?"

"Woman," said M. Goron weightily, "is incalculable."

"But surely not as incalculable as all that?"

This time M. Goron took a slower, longer measurement of the hall as he paced it. His head was down, and he fumed. Several times he began to speak, but checked himself. At last he spread out his hands in exasperation.

"My friend," he cried, "you try to persuade me flat against the evidence!"

"Yet one has doubts?"

"One," the prefect confessed, "sometimes has doubts."

"You are still going to arrest her?"

M. Goron was astonished. "Naturally! There is no question but that the examining magistrate will order it. Unless, of course —" his eye had a sardonic twinkle, "— my good friend the doctor can demonstrate her innocence within the next few hours. Tell me. Have you a theory about this?"

"In a way, I have a theory."

"Which is?"

Again Dermot looked him straight in the eyes.

"It seems to me almost certain," he replied, "that the murder was committed by some member of this 'pleasant' Lawes family."

XI

IT REQUIRED a great deal to startle the prefect of police of La Bandelette. This did it. His eyes seemed to bulge as he stared back at his companion. After a pause, as though gestures alone would suffice for such an incredible proposition, he pointed his finger inquiringly at the closed door of the drawing room.

"Yes," said Dermot. "I mean just that."

M. Goron cleared his throat.

"You wished, I think, to see the room where the crime was committed. Come with me, and you shall see it. Until then —" he made a frantic pantomime of calling for silence, "— not another word!"

And M. Goron swept round and led the way up the stairs. Dermot could hear him groaning.

The hall on the floor above was also dark until M. Goron switched on the lights. He indicated the door of the study, at the front. Tall and white-painted, it was a door to riddles; it might become a door to terror. Bracing himself, Dermot laid hold of the metal handle, and pushed it open.

A blur of twilight lay beyond. Fitted carpet, like that of the study, is rare in French houses; this carpet was so thick that the bottom of the door clung to it and scraped the nap as it swung. Dermot's mind registered the fact as he groped to the left of the door after a light switch.

There were two light switches, one above the other. When he pressed the first, it kindled the desk-lamp in its green-glass shade, on the flat-topped table desk. When he pressed the second, the central chandelier with its flashing prisms, a sort of glass castle, sprang into blaze.

He saw a square room, its wood-panelled walls glistening white. Immediately opposite him were the two long windows, steel shutters now closed. In the wall to (his) left was the heavy white marble mantelpiece. Against the wall to his right stood the table desk, its swivel-chair pushed a little way out. The spindly gilt-and-brocade chairs, the little round-topped gilt table in the center, stood out colorfully against gray carpet. All round the walls, except where one or two bookcases broke their line, glass-fronted curio cabinets reflected back the glitter of the chandelier. At any other time their exhibits would have intrigued him.

The room was stuffy. It smelled strongly of some cleaning fluid, like the smell of death itself.

Dermot walked over to the desk.

Yes: much cleaning had been done here. Old blood stains, now rust-brown, remained only on the

desk blotter and on the large writing pad where Sir
Maurice Lawes had been making notes just before
his death.

No traces of the shattered snuff-box remained. A
magnifying glass, a jeweler's lens, pens, ink, and
other desk-materials were scattered over the blotter,
under the light of the green-glass lamp. Dermot
glanced at the writing pad, beside which a gold
fountain-pen had dropped from its owner's hand.
The writing on the pad was headed in very large,
ornamental, neat lettering, "Snuff-box, shaped like a
watch, once the property of the Emperor Napoleon
I." Then, in small but meticulously neat copperplate
script, it went on:

> *This snuff-box was presented to Bonaparte by
> his father-in-law, the Emperor of Austria, at the
> birth of Napoleon's son, the King of Rome,
> March 20th, 1811. The case measures 2¼ inches
> in diameter. It is bound in gold; the dummy
> watch-stem is of gold; the watch-numerals and
> hands are made of small diamonds, with Bona-
> parte's crest, the letter "N" in the centre of—*

Here the writing ended in two splashes of blood.
Dermot whistled. "This thing," he said, "must
have been enormously valuable!"

"Valuable?" the prefect almost screamed. "Haven't I told you?"

"Yet it was smashed."

"As you see, dear doctor." M. Goron pointed. "I also told you it was of curious shape. As you will see by the writing, it was shaped like a watch."

"What sort of watch?"

"An ordinary watch!" M. Goron fished out his own and held it up. "In point of fact, the members of the family tell me, when Sir Maurice first showed it to them they thought it *was* a watch. It opened out . . . so. Kindly note the nicks in the wood on the desk where the murderer's blows went wild."

Dermot put down the note pad.

While the prefect watched him in an agony of doubt, he turned round and looked across the room at the stand of fire irons beside the marble mantelpiece. Over this mantelpiece hung a bronze medallion profile of the Emperor Napoleon. The poker with which the crime had been committed was now missing from the stand of fire irons. Dermot measured distances with his eye. His mind clashed and rang with half-formed ideas, out of which there emerged at least one inconsistency in the evidence given by M. Goron.

"Tell me," he said. "Is any member of the Lawes family afflicted with bad eyesight?"

"Ah, my God!" cried M. Goron, and threw up his hands. "The Lawes family! Always the Lawes family! Look here." He grew more subdued. "We are alone now. Nobody can hear us. Will you tell me why you are so positive that one of them must have murdered the old man?"

"I persist in my question. Is any of the family afflicted with bad eyesight?"

"That, dear doctor, I can't say."

"But it should be easy to find out?"

"Undoubtedly!" M. Goron hesitated. His eyes narrowed. "You were thinking," he suggested, and made the motion of one who strikes with a poker, "that the murderer must have had bad eyesight to miss a target like a human head with some of his blows?"

"Perhaps."

Dermot made a slow tour of the room, peering into the glass cases. Some of the exhibits stood in lonely splendor, others were ticketed with neat cards in the same tiny copperplate writing. Though he had no knowledge of collecting beyond some acquaintance with precious stones, it would have been apparent to anyone that this hodge-podge contained a large quantity of merely interesting junk mixed with a number of genuinely fine items.

There was porcelain, there were fans, reliquaries,

an extraordinary clock or two, a rack of Toledo rapiers, and one case (grim and dingy amid delicate knick-knacks) devoted to relics obtained at the demolition of old Newgate prison. In the bookcases Dermot noted that a greater part of the books were technical works dealing with the identification of jewels.

"To continue?" persisted M. Goron.

"There was one other bit of evidence you mentioned," said Dermot. "You told me that, though nothing had been stolen, a diamond-and-turquoise necklace had been taken from one of the cabinets. You found it, slightly bloodstained, lying on the floor under the cabinet."

M. Goron nodded, and tapped a bulbous glass cabinet immediately to the left of the door. Like the others, this cabinet was not locked. Its front swung smoothly open at the touch of M. Goron's finger. The shelves inside were made of glass. Occupying the place of honor in the center, against a background of dark-blue velvet tilted up so as to be seen better, the necklace burned with shifting fires against the prism-dazzle of the chandelier.

"It has been replaced, and wiped clean," M. Goron said. "By tradition, this necklace was worn by Madame de Lamballe, the favorite of Queen Marie-Antoinette, when Madame was hacked to death by the mob outside the prison of La Force. — Sir Maurice Lawes had a curious taste for the gruesome, don't you think?"

"Someone has a curious taste for the gruesome."

M. Goron chuckled. "You observe what stands beside it?"

"It looks," said Dermot, glancing to the left of the necklace, "like a music-box on little wheels."

"It *is* a music-box on little wheels. And, faith, it was bad judgment to put that music-box on a glass shelf. I remember, the day following the crime, when we were examining this room with the dead man still sitting in his chair, that the commissaire of police opened this case. His hand struck the music-box. It fell on the floor. . . ."

Again M. Goron pointed to the box, a very heavy one of wood on whose dingy tin sides were painted faded scenes of what Dermot recognized as the American Civil War.

"The music-box landed on its side. It began to play *John Brown's Body*. You have heard the tune?" The prefect whistled a few bars of it. "Its effect, I assure you, was remarkable. M. Horatio Lawes angrily flies out and tells us not to touch his father's collection. M. Benjamin Phillips says somebody must have been playing the music-box recently; since he, a mechanician of talent, repaired it and wound it up only a few days before, and now it runs down after playing a stave or two. Can you imagine such a commotion over a small point of the sort."

"Yes, I think I can. As I told you earlier today, this is a characteristic crime."

"Ah!" M. Goron leaped to attention. "I know you did. It would interest me very much to hear why you said that."

"Because," answered Dermot, "this is a domestic crime. A cozy, comfortable, hearth-rug murder of the sort which almost always originates at home."

M. Goron passed an unsteady hand across his forehead. He glanced round him as though seeking inspiration.

"Doctor," he said, "are you serious?"

Dermot sat down on the edge of the center table. He ran his fingers through the thick dark hair that was parted on one side. He seemed groping to arrange his eyes, while the dark eyes had an almost crackling effect in their intensity.

"Here's a man beaten to death with nine blows of a poker when one would have sufficed. You look at it. And you say, 'This is brutal; it is senseless; it is almost the work of a madman.' Therefore you turn away from the quiet domestic circle, where you assume that no person can have acted so savagely.

"But that's not the history of crime. Certainly not

of Anglo-Saxon crime, which I quote because these people are English. The ordinary murderer, with a cold and definite motive, seldom acts with such brutality. Why should he? His business, for a clear purpose, is to kill as neatly and cleanly as he can.

"It is usually *at home* — where emotions have to be stifled because people must live together, where domestic conditions gradually grow more intolerable — that you see the climax suddenly burst in an outbreak of such violence that we ordinary people can't believe it. Affect the domestic emotions, and you produce a motive whose outlet stuns the mind.

"Should you say, offhand, that a well-brought-up woman in the most pious of households would kill first her stepmother and then her own father with repeated blows of a hatchet, for no apparent reason except vague family friction? Does a middle-aged insurance agent, who has never in his life exchanged a cross word with his wife, batter in her skull with a poker? Does a quiet girl of sixteen cut the throat of her baby brother, merely because she resents the presence of her stepmother? You don't believe it? There's not enough motive? Yet these things happened."

"To monsters, perhaps," said M. Goron.

"On the contrary, to ordinary persons like you or me. As for Mrs. Neill . . ."

"Ah! What have we there?"

"Mrs. Neill," returned Dermot, keeping his eyes fixed steadily on his companion, "saw something. Don't ask me what! She knows it is one of the members of this household."

"Then why, in the name of a name, doesn't she speak out?"

"She may not know which one."

M. Goron shook his head with a satiric smile.

"Doctor, I don't find that good enough. Nor do I find much to favor in your psychology."

Dermot took out a packet of yellow Maryland cigarettes. He lit one with a pocket lighter, closed the lighter with a snap, and regarded M. Goron with eyes which the prefect found more than a little disquieting. Dermot was smiling, yet with no pleasure in it except the pleasure of a theory verified. He inhaled smoke and blew out a cloud of it under the bright light.

"By evidence which you have told me yourself," he said, in that deep and level voice which he could make almost hypnotic, "one of the members of the Lawes family has told a deliberate, flat, provable lie." He paused. "Will you think twice about it if I tell you what the lie is?"

M. Goron moistened his lips.

But he had no time to reply. The door to the hall

— Dermot, in fact, was already pointing to the door as though to indicate what he meant — swung open. Janice Lawes, shielding her eyes with her hand, peered in.

The room, obviously, still frightened her. She gave a quick glance, like a child, at the empty swivel chair; her body seemed to stiffen as she caught the ugly cleansing smell of the room; but she came in quietly, and closed the door. Standing with her back to it, her dark frock outlined against the white panel, she addressed Dermot in English.

"I couldn't think where you'd got to," she said accusingly. "You went out into the hall, and then you — pfft!" She made a gesture intended to represent disappearance.

"Yes, mademoiselle?" prompted M. Goron.

Janice ignored him, and addressed herself to Dermot. She seemed to be nerving herself for an outburst. But it was only after a long silence, while her moving eyes searched his face, that the outburst came with its own youthful directness.

"You think we're being beastly to Eve, don't you?"

Dermot smiled at her.

"I thought you stood up for her nobly, Miss Lawes." Though he tried to guard against it, he found his jaws shutting together and wrath burning like a fire whenever he thought of a certain expression. "But your brother, on the other hand . . ."

"You don't *understand* Toby," cried Janice, and stamped her foot.

"Maybe not."

"Toby's in love with her. Toby's a straightforward soul with a single code of morals."

"Sancta simplicitas!"

"That means, 'sacred simplicity,' doesn't it?" Janice asked directly. She eyed him. She was trying with desperation to hold on to her usual flippancy, and not succeeding. "It's no odds to me. But I wish you'd try to see our side of it too. After all —" She pointed to the swivel chair.

"He's dead," Janice went on. "That's the only thing any of us can think of. When you have a thing like that accusation sprung on you all of a sudden, you don't just say, 'Of course I'm sure there's nothing in this; why bother even to explain?' You wouldn't be human if you did."

In fairness, Dermot had to admit this was true. He smiled at her. It seemed to give her courage.

"That was why," Janice continued, "I wanted to ask you a question. In confidence. It *will* be in confidence, won't it?"

"Of course!" M. Goron interposed smoothly, before Dermot could reply. "Er — where is Mrs. Neill now?"

Janice's face clouded.

"She's having it out with Toby. Mother and Uncle Ben discreetly cleared off. But this question I wanted to ask." She hesitated. Then she drew a deep breath, looking full at Dermot. "You remember, a while ago you and Mother were discussing how Daddy was interested in — prison work?"

For some reason, the last two words struck a chord of ugliness.

"Yes?" said Dermot.

"That's what brought it back to me. You also remember, there's been a lot of talk about the queer way Daddy looked on the afternoon of the night he was killed? How he came back from his walk, and wouldn't go to the theatre, and he looked as white as a ghost and his hand shook? While you were talking, I remembered the only time I've ever seen him look like that before."

"Well?"

"About eight years ago," said Janice, "there was a smooth, oily old bloke named Finisterre, who got him interested in a business deal, and swindled him. I don't know the details; I wasn't very old then, or much interested in business. Any more than I am now, for that matter. But I do remember the awful rumpus it created."

M. Goron, who had been following this by

cupping one hand behind his ear, was puzzled.

"This may be very interesting," the prefect said. "But, frankly, I fail to see . . ."

"Wait!" Janice appealed to Dermot. "Daddy hadn't a good memory for faces. But he would remember sometimes, when he least expected it. While 'Finisterre' was talking to him — there wasn't any legal redress for the swindle, you see — he suddenly remembered who the man was.

" 'Finisterre' was a convict named McConklin, who'd got out on ticket-of-leave and then jumped his parole and disappeared. Daddy'd been interested in this case, though McConklin had never seen him: at least, to know who he was. Then up McConklin pops out of the blue.

"When McConklin, or Finisterre, saw he was recognized, he wept and begged and pleaded not to be handed over to the police again. He offered to return the money. He talked about his wife and children. He offered to do anything, *anything*, if only Daddy wouldn't send him back to jail. Mother says Daddy was as white as a ghost, and went up and was sick in the bathroom. Because he hated, he honestly hated, locking up a criminal. But that didn't mean he wouldn't do it. I think he'd have jailed one of his own family, if he thought something really indefensible had been done."

Janice paused.

She had been speaking in a rapid monotone, her lips dry. She kept looking round the room, as though she might still find her father's presence among the curio cabinets.

"So he said to Finisterre, 'I'll give you twenty-four hours to make yourself scarce. At the end of that time, whether you've done it or not, a full account of you in your new life — where you're to be found in your new life — your new name — everything about you — goes to Scotland Yard.' And he did it. Finisterre died in jail. Mother says that Daddy could hardly eat a mouthful for days afterwards. You see, he *liked* the man."

Janice put both conviction and significance into those last words.

"I don't want you to believe I'm a little cat. I'm not, I'm not, I'm not! That is: I don't mean to be, whatever I happen to sound like. But it's no good saying it didn't occur to me." Again she looked Dermot in the eyes. "Do you think Eve Neill has ever been in prison?"

XII

IN THE drawing room downstairs, Eve and Toby had the place to themselves. Only one standard-lamp, with a golden-yellow shade, had been turned on; and this in a far corner of the room. Neither of them wanted to have a good look at the other's face.

Eve was searching for her handbag, which in the present muddled state of her wits she could not find. She kept walking aimlessly round the room, examining the same places over and over; but, as she seemed to be approaching the door, Toby hurried to it and stood in front of it.

"You're not going?" he demanded.

"I want my handbag," Eve said blindly. "Then I must go. Will you stand away from that door, please?"

"But we've got to talk this thing out!"

"What is there to talk about?"

"The police think —"

"The police, as you heard," Eve told him, "are coming to arrest me. So I'd better go over and pack a bag, hadn't I? They'll allow me that, I hope."

A baffled expression crossed Toby's face. He put

up one hand and rubbed his forehead. Justice must be done: he did not realize how self-consciously noble he looked, how martyr-like and heroic, with his chin up and an obvious determination to do the right thing whatever it cost his feelings.

"You understand," he said, "I'll stand by you. Don't for a minute think I won't!"

"Thank you."

Sensing no irony, Toby kept a thoughtful eye on the floor. He had begun to reflect.

"Whatever happens, they mustn't arrest you. That's the great thing. I doubt if they mean it anyway. They're probably bluffing. But I'll see the British Consul tonight. You see, if they arrested you — well, the bank wouldn't like it."

"I hope none of you would like it."

"You don't understand these things, Eve. Hockson's is one of the oldest financial institutions in England. And Caesar's wife and all that, as I've often said before. You mustn't blame me just because I try to safeguard our position."

Eve held tight to her nerves.

"Do you believe I killed your father, Toby?"

She was surprised at the look of shrewdness which animated his rather stolid features, a flash of something deeper than she had ever noticed in Toby Lawes.

"You never killed anybody," he retorted. His forehead darkened. "That damned maid of yours is behind all this, or I'm a Dutchman. She —"

"What do you know about her, Toby?"

"Nothing." He drew a deep breath. "But I do think it's a little hard on me," — the querulous note rose in his voice, — "just when we were getting on so well, and everything was so pleasant, that you should pick up with this Atwood fellow again."

"Is that what you believe?"

Toby was in agony.

"What else can I believe? Come on, now: let's be honest! Mind you, I'm not quite so old-fashioned as you think, in spite of Janice's joking. In fact, I flatter myself I'm pretty broad-minded. I don't know, or want to know, anything about your past life before you met me. I can forgive and forget all that."

Eve stopped short, and merely looked at him.

"But, hang it all," Toby went on heatedly, "a man has certain ideals. Yes, ideals! And, when he's going to marry a girl, he expects her to live up to those ideals."

Eve found her handbag. It was lying on a conspicuous table, in plain sight; she wondered why she had passed it by so many times before. She picked it up, snapped it open, and automatically looked inside. Then she made her way to the door.

"Get out of the way, please. I want to go."

"Look here, you can't go now! Suppose you ran into police, or even reporters, or somebody? In your present condition, Lord knows what you might say."

"And Hookson's wouldn't like that?"

"Well, it's no good saying that doesn't matter. We've got to be realists about this, Eve. That's what you women won't understand."

"It's nearly dinner time, you know."

"But I could even — yes, I could even go so far as this! I could almost tell Hookson's to go to the devil, if only I could be sure of just one thing. *Are* you playing straight with me, after I've played straight with you? Have you taken up with Atwood again?"

"No."

"I don't believe you."

"Then," said Eve, "why bother to keep asking me the same question, over and over? — Will you stand out of the way, please?"

"Oh, very well," said Toby, and folded his arms with outraged dignity. "If that's how you feel about it."

He stood aside, with meticulous and careful pacing, and an air of detached courtesy. His chin was in the air. Eve hesitated. She was in love with him; she would reassure him another time; but even his obvious anguish, so flamboyant because it was so real, could not shake her now. She ran past him into the foyer, and closed the door behind her.

The bright lights of the foyer momentarily blinded her. When she had adjusted her eyes to them, she found Uncle Ben Phillips bearing down on her and making noises in his throat.

"Hullo!" said Uncle Ben. "Leaving?"

(*Not another one! Please, dear God, not another one!*)

Uncle Ben had the embarrassed manner of one who wants to sneak up and impart sympathy without being seen. With one hand he scratched his grizzled head. In the other he was carrying, as though he did not know what to do with it, a somewhat crumpled envelope.

"Er — almost forgot," he added. "Letter for you."

"For me?"

Uncle Ben nodded towards the front door. "Found it in the letter box ten minutes ago. Delivered by hand, evidently. Your name on it, though." The gentle, ice-blue eyes fixed on her. "Might be important?"

Eve didn't care whether or not it was important. She took the letter, glanced at her name written across the envelope, and thrust it into her handbag. Uncle Ben put an empty pipe into his mouth and

sucked at it noisily; he seemed, by internal strug-
glings, to be winding himself up for speech.

"I don't amount to much in this house," he observed abruptly. "But — I'm on your side."

"Thanks."

"Always!" said Uncle Ben. But, when he reached
out to touch her arm, she instinctively flinched and
the slow-moving old man stiffened as though she had
struck him in the face. "Anything wrong, my dear?"

"No. Sorry!"

"Like the gloves, eh?"

"What gloves?"

"You know," said Uncle Ben, again fixing his mild
eyes on her face. "When I was working with the
car, and had brown gloves on. I only wondered why
it worried you."

Eve turned and ran.

Out in the street, it was just dark: a mellow evening of that September weather which seems more
exhilarating than spring. The pale white of street
lamps had kindled among chestnut trees. Eve seemed
to come out into a free world, after the stifling atmosphere of the Villa Bonheur. But it was not, for her,
likely to remain a free world much longer.

Brown gloves. Brown gloves. Brown gloves.

She went out of the gate, and stopped in the
shadow of the wall. She wanted to be by herself;

alone as though shut into a box; away from insinuat-
ing voices and probing eyes, where nobody could see
her for the dark.

You *fool*, she said to herself. Why didn't you come
out and tell them what you'd seen? Why didn't you
say that somebody in that house, wearing a pair of
brown gloves, was an unctuous hypocrite? You
couldn't speak, couldn't force the words through
your throat; but why not? Loyalty to them? A fear
that they would recoil still more from you at such
an accusation? Or mere loyalty to Toby, who whatever his faults was at least honest and straightforward?

But you owe one of them no loyalty, Eve Neill.
Not an ounce. Not now.

It was the crocodile tears that sickened Eve most.
You couldn't hold the whole family guilty. All but
one were as shocked and bewildered as she. But somebody, who turned reproachful eyes on Eve, had
been able to commit murder as coldly as mix a
salad.

And all of them — if you came to the root of the
matter, this was what stirred the deepest anger in
Eve's heart — all of them had been only too ready to
believe her a kind of casual harlot, whom they were
being so damned broad-minded about graciously
pardoning. It wasn't as bad as this, perhaps. They

were upset. They had a right to be. But it was the patronage Eve hated.

And in the meantime?

Prison, evidently.

This couldn't be! It wasn't happening!

Only two persons, whether by accident or design, had shown a decency which warmed her to them. One was the despised rake Ned Atwood, who never professed to be "nice," but who had collapsed telling a lie which he thought would shield her. The other was that doctor. She couldn't remember his name. For the life of her she couldn't even remember what he looked like. Yet she remembered his expression, the twinkling dark eyes with a hatred of hypocrisy behind them; the sense of intelligence like a sword, of a bubble burst and a posturing collapsed when his ironic voice rang in the Lawes's drawing room.

The question was, would the police believe Ned Atwood even when Ned told the simple truth?

Ned was ill, he was hurt, he was unconscious. "Not expected to recover." In her own danger, she was forgetting his. Could she be of any use if she threw her bonnet over the windmill, defying the whole tribe of Lawes, and went to Ned? At the moment she couldn't even telephone, or write him a letter. . . .

Letter.

Standing in the cool shadow of the rue des Anges,

Eve's fingers closed round her handbag. She opened the bag, and peered at the rather crumpled envelope inside.

Eve crossed the rue des Anges with a firm stride, and stopped under the street lamp not far from her own gate. She examined the gray envelope, sealed, with her name written across it in small French script. Delivered by hand, dropped into the letter box of a house where she did not live. There could be nothing either formidable or sinister about an ordinary envelope. Yet Eve felt the slow, hard beating of her heart, and a warmth coming up into her throat, as she tore it open. The brief note inside was in French, unsigned.

> *If madame wishes to learn something which will be of value to her in her present predicament, let her call at number 17, rue de la Harpe, at any time after ten o'clock. The door is open. Please to enter.*

Overhead, the leaves whispered. They threw wavering shadows across the gray paper.

Eve raised her eyes. Ahead of her was her own villa, where Yvette Latour waited to prepare her dinner in the absence of the cook. Eve folded up the note, and put it back in her handbag.

She had hardly touched the doorbell before Yvette, as competent and expressionless as ever, opened the door from inside.

"Madame's dinner is ready," Yvette told her. "It has been ready this half-hour."

"I don't want any dinner."

"But madame must have some dinner. It is necessary to keep one's strength up."

"Why?" said Eve.

She had been walking towards the stairs, brushing past her companion, in the bright little jewel-box of a hall with its clocks and mirrors. Now she turned round, and flung out the question. Never had she been so conscious of the fact that she and Yvette were alone in the house.

"I said, why?" repeated Eve.

"Faith, madame," returned Yvette, with an unexpected crow of good-nature which avoided the challenge. Yvette's eyes widened. She put her hands, as strong as a wrestler's, on her hips. "It is necessary for all of us to keep up our strength in this life. Isn't it?"

"Why did you lock me out of the house on the night Sir Maurice Lawes was killed?"

Now you could distinctly hear the ticking of the clocks.

"Madame?"

"You heard me!"

"I heard madame. But I did not comprehend her."

"What have you told the police about me?" demanded Eve. She felt her heart contract and her cheeks begin to burn.

"Madame?"

"Why hasn't my white lace negligée come back from the cleaner's?"

"Alas, madame! I can't say. Sometimes they take an interminable while, don't they? — When will madame have her dinner?"

The challenge, dropped, was shattered like one of Sir Maurice Lawes's porcelain plates.

"I tell you I don't want any dinner," said Eve, with her foot on the first tread of the stairs. "I am going to my room."

"I may perhaps bring madame some sandwiches?"

"Yes, if you like. And some coffee."

"*Bien*, madame. Will madame be going out again tonight?"

"Perhaps. I don't know."

And she ran up the stairs.

In her bedroom, the damask curtains had been drawn and the light turned on over the dressing-table. Eve closed the door. She was short of breath; there seemed to be a large hollow inside her chest, where a small pulse beat; her knees felt shaky and the blood now seemed to be in her head rather than her cheeks. Dropping into an easy chair, she tried to relax.

Number 17, rue de la Harpe. Number 17, rue de la Harpe. Number 17, rue de la Harpe.

There was no clock in the bedroom. Eve slipped down the hall, to a spare room, and brought one. It seemed to tick as menacingly as a bomb. She put it on the chest of drawers, and then went into the bathroom to wash her hands and face. When she returned, a plate of sandwiches and a pot of filtered coffee had been set out neatly on a side table. Though she could eat nothing, she drank some coffee and smoked many cigarettes while the hands of the clock crawled from eight-thirty to nine, and from nine-thirty towards ten.

She had attended a trial for murder once, at Paris. Ned had taken her, thinking it all a good joke. What had surprised her was the amount of shouting. The judges — there were several of them, wearing bibs and flat-topped caps — stormed at the prisoner as much as did the prosecuting counsel, exhorting him to confess.

At the time it had seemed foreign and unpleasantly funny. But it wasn't funny for the grimy-faced wretch on trial, gripping the edge of the dock with black nails, and screaming back at them. When they brought him into court, two locks clanged on a door opening into a passage that smelled of creosote. A whiff of it came back to Eve. It suggested what might happen. She was so absorbed in these images that she hardly heard the noises in the street below.

But she heard the doorbell ring.

There was a mutter of voices downstairs. On the stairs Eve heard the pad, pad, pad of feet on carpet, as Yvette mounted those steps faster than she had ever done before. Yvette knocked at the bedroom door. Yvette remained respectful.

"There are many policemen downstairs, madame," she reported. The sheer joyousness of her tone, the naked satisfaction as at a task well done, turned Eve's mouth dry. "Shall I tell them that madame will be down to see them?"

That voice rang in Eve's ears for several seconds after the other had ceased to speak.

"Put them in the front drawing room," Eve heard herself saying. "I shall be down in one moment."

"*Bien*, madame."

Eve got to her feet as the door closed. She went to the wardrobe and took out a short fur wrap, which she fastened round her neck. She looked in her hand-bag to make sure that she had money. Then she switched off the light and slipped out into the hall.

Avoiding the loose stair-rod, she ran downstairs so lightly that no one heard her. She had timed

Yvette's progress as though she had been able to imagine every move. The mutter of voices now proceeded from the front drawing room; the door was only partly open and Yvette's back turned, hand raised in a gesture of hospitality to the law. Though Eve caught one brief glimpse of an eye and a mustache, she did not believe she had been seen. Two seconds more, and she was out through the dark dining room to the even darker kitchen.

Again, as on another occasion, she unfastened the spring lock of the back door. But this time she closed it behind her. She ascended the steps to the dew-wet back garden, while the beam of the inland lighthouse swung overhead. She hurried out of the back gate into the lane. Three minutes later — having disturbed nothing except a frantic dog chained in somebody's garden — she was hailing a taxi in the dim stateliness of the Boulevard du Casino.

"Number seventeen, rue de la Harpe," said Eve.

XIII

"THIS is it?"

"Yes, madame," said the taxi-driver. "Number seventeen, rue de la Harpe."

"It is a private house?"

"No, madame. It is a shop. A flower-shop."

The street, it developed, was to be found in the un-fashionable part of La Bandelette: that is to say, close to the promenade and the sea-front. Most of the English money-spinners who patronized La Bandelette used to be very scornful of this district, because it looked (and was) exactly like Weston or Paignton or Folkestone.

By day it throbbed, gray and slaty, a hive of small streets and shops struck with souvenir-colors, bristling in toy spades and buckets and windmills, yellow Kodak-signs, decorous family bars. But at night, as autumn lengthened, most of these streets turned lightless and damp. The rue de la Harpe, curving between tall houses, swallowed up the taxi. When the cab drew up before a dark shop-front, Eve felt a panic reluctance to get out.

She sat with her hand on the half-open door, looking at the driver in the dim glow of the meter-lamp.

"A — a flower shop?" she repeated.

"Veritably, madame." The driver pointed to white enamel lettering just visible against the dim shop-window. " 'At the Garden of Paradise. Choice Blooms Sold Here.' It is closed, you understand," he added helpfully.

"So I see."

"Would madame wish me to take her somewhere else?"

"No. This will do." Eve climbed out. Still she hesitated. "You don't happen to know who owns the shop, do you?"

"Ah! The owner. No," said the driver, after giving this careful consideration. "As to the owner, I can't say. But the patronne I know very well indeed. The patronne is Mademoiselle Latour. Mademoiselle Prue for short. A very genteel young lady."

"*Latour?*"

"Yes, madame. Is madame unwell?"

"No! Has she a relation, a sister or aunt perhaps, named Yvette Latour?"

The driver stared at her.

"My word, now, but that's too big an order! I regret, madame, that I can't say. Only the shop I know, which is spick-and-span and pretty like mademoiselle herself." (Here Eve felt curious eyes fixed on her in the gloom). "Would madame wish that I wait here for her?"

"No. Yes! Yes, perhaps you'd better."

Though she started to ask another question, Eve thought better of it. She turned round abruptly and hurried across the pavement to the flower shop.

Behind her the impassive taxi-driver was thinking:

My God, but that is a very pretty piece, and clearly English! Is it possible, now, that Mademoiselle Prue may have been playing about with madame's boy-friend, and madame comes here to execute vengeance? In that case, Marcel old man, one had better let in one's clutch and scram out of here quickly, in case there is vitriol-throwing. Come to think, however, the English do not often throw vitriol. But they have formidable tempers, as I have seen when meester gets drunk and missus *se parle de ça.* Yes: one foresees something rather pleasant and interesting without being lethal. And, besides, she owes me eight francs forty.

Eve's own thoughts were less simply straightforward than these.

She paused outside the shop door. Beside it was the clean, polished plate-glass window, beyond which little could be seen. The edge of a moon showed over dark roof-tops, but it was reflected in the window and rendered the glass opaque.

Any time after ten o'clock. The door is open. Please to enter.

Eve turned the knob, and found the door open. She pushed it wide, expecting momentarily to hear the ping of a bell above it. Still nothing happened. Silence, and darkness. Leaving the door wide open, not without strong fears as to what this might mean but reassured by the presence of the taxi-driver in the street outside, Eve entered the shop.

Still nothing. . . .

Cool, moist, fragrant air blew out at her, settling round as she passed. It did not appear to be a large shop. Close against the window, a covered bird cage hung on a chain from the low ceiling. The edge of moonlight lay along the floor, showing only the ghostliness of a flower-bedizened room and raising on one wall the shadow of a funeral-wreath.

She had passed a counter and cash register, among mingled flower scents thinned by damp as though by water, before she noticed a crack of yellow light at the back of the shop. It lay along the floor under a heavy portière which closed off the doorway to a rear room. And, at the same moment, a girl's sprightly voice sang out from behind the portière.

"Who is there?" the voice called in French.

Eve walked forward, and drew aside the portière.

The only word to describe that scene was domesticity. The place oozed domesticity. She was looking into a small, snug sitting-room, the walls papered in regrettable taste but breathing of home.

The mantelpiece consisted of many wooden pigeon holes built round a mirror, and in the grate burned a bright fire of those round coals which the French call *boulets*. There was a fringed lamp on the center table. There was a sofa, with dolls. Over the piano hung a framed family-group photograph.

Mademoiselle Prue herself, composed and agreeable, sat in an easy chair by the lamp. Eve had never seen her before, but M. Goron or Dermot Kinross would have recognized her. She was dressed in very good taste, and had extraordinary poise. Her large, dark, demure eyes were raised to Eve. A sewing-basket stood on the table beside her; at the moment she was engaged in biting off a thread, as she mended a seam of the pink elastic suspender-belt in her hands. It was this more than anything else which gave the scene its air of cozy domesticity and slippered ease.

Across from her sat Toby Lawes.

Mademoiselle Prue rose to her feet, putting down needle, thread, and suspender-belt.

"Ah, madame!" she said briskly. "You have received my note, then? That is good. Please come in."

There was a long silence.

Eve's first impulse, it is regrettable to state, was to laugh in Toby's face. But this wasn't funny. It wasn't funny at all.

Toby sat rigid. He looked back at Eve as though he were fascinated, and could not avoid her eye. Color, dull red, slowly suffused his face until it seemed bursting; if you had wanted an index of his conscience, you could read it, with a clearness painful to watch, in every line of his expression. Any man who saw him then would have felt almost sorry for him.

Eve thought: At any minute, now, I am going to get good and mad. But for the moment I can't. I can't.

"You — you wrote that note?" she heard herself saying.

"I regret!" replied Prue, with an anxious smile and real concern. "But, madame, it is necessary to be practical."

She went over to Toby and kissed him perfunctorily on the forehead.

"This poor Toby," she said. "I have been his little friend for such a long time, yet I cannot seem to make him understand. And now it is necessary to speak frankly. Yes?"

"Yes," said Eve. "By all means."

Prue's pretty face again became composed and self assured.

"Madame, look you, I am no daughter of joy! I am a young girl of good character and family." She pointed to the photograph over the piano. "That is my papa. That is my mama. That is my Uncle Arsène. That is my sister Yvette. If I am sometimes entrapped into a moment of weakness . . . well! Is that not the privilege of every woman who considers herself human?"

Eve looked at Toby.

Toby started to get up, but sat down again.

"But mark you!" said Prue. "It was understood . . . or at least *I* so understood it, in my innocence . . . that M. Lawes's intentions were honorable and that he meant marriage. Then comes the announcement of his betrothal to you. No, no, no, no!" Her voice grew hollow with reproach. "I ask you! Was that fair? Was it just? Was it honorable?"

She shrugged her shoulders.

"Still, I knew these men! My sister Yvette, she is furious. She says *she* will find a way to break off this marriage and put me in the arms of M. Lawes."

"Is that true, now?" said Eve, now beginning to understand many things.

"But me, I am not like that. I run after nobody. *Je m'en fous de ca*! If this Tobee is cold, there are other fish in the sea. But it is only fair, I say — and madame as a woman will agree with me — that some small compensation should be made to me for my loss of time and the violation of my natural feelings. Yes?"

Toby found his voice.

"You wrote her a note . . . ?" he began in a dazed voice.

Prue paid no attention to him, beyond giving him an absent-mindedly affectionate smile. Her real business was with Eve.

"I ask him please if he will give me this compensation, so that we can part friends. I wish him well. I congratulate him on his marriage. But he puts me off, saying that he is hard up."

Prue's glance showed what she thought of this.

"Then his papa dies. That is very sad," — Prue looked honestly concerned,—"and for almost a week I do not trouble him, except to express my sympathy. Besides, he says that as his papa's heir he will now be able to deal generously with me. But mark! Only yesterday he says that his papa's affairs of business are in a mess; that there is not much money; and that my neighbor, M. Veille the art-dealer, presses for payment on a broken snuff-box costing, incredible to imagine, seven hundred and fifty thousand francs."

"This note . . ." Toby began.

Still Prue addressed herself to Eve.

"Yes, I wrote it," she acknowledged. "My sister

Yvette does not know that I wrote it. It is an idea of my own."

"Why did you write it?" said Eve.

"Madame, can you ask?"

"I do ask."

"To anyone of sensibility," said Prue, with pouting reproach, "it is apparent." She went over and smoothed Toby's hair. "I am very fond of this poor Tobee . . ."

The gentleman in question jumped to his feet.

"And, faith, I am not rich. Though I think you will admit," explained Prue, teetering on her toes to survey herself complacently in the mirror over the fireplace, "that I turn myself out rather well for all that. *Hein*?"

"Beautifully!"

"Well! Madame *is* rich, or so they tell me. Surely persons of sensibility, of refinement, should comprehend these things without diagrams?"

"I still don't. . . ."

"Madame wishes to marry my poor Tobee. Desolated as I am to lose him, I am what you call a good sport. I am independent. I interfere with nobody. But in these things, *voyons*, it is necessary to be practical. Therefore if madame herself would consent to make some small compensation, I am sure that matters could be adjusted with the best will in the world."

Again there was a long silence.

"Why does madame start to laugh?" demanded Prue, in a different and sharper voice.

"I beg your pardon. I wasn't laughing. That is — not really. May I sit down?"

"But of course! How I am forgetting my manners! Here: have this chair. It is Tobee's favorite."

All the scarlet of embarrassment, and mortification at being caught here, had faded out of Toby's face. He no longer resembled such a seething picture of guilt, dazed-eyed like a boxer at the end of the fifteenth round, that you wanted to slap him on the back and say, "it's all right, old man."

He still carried himself stiffly. But wrath was asserting itself, and self-righteousness too. Human nature remains human nature, whether we like it or not. He had got himself into an embarrassing position. Therefore he was going to take it out on somebody — perhaps on anybody — for being put in that position.

"Get out," he said to Prue.

"Monsieur?"

"*I said, get out!*"

"Aren't you forgetting," interposed Eve, with such cold and rapid effect that Toby blinked, "aren't you forgetting this is Mademoiselle Latour's house?"

"I don't care whose house it is. I mean . . ."

With a violent effort Toby got control of himself, after pushing his hands through his hair and seeming to hold hard to his skull. He straightened up, breathing hard.

"Get out of here," he requested. "Please. Scoot. *Va-t'en*. I wish to speak to madame."

The cloud of anxiety had lifted from Prue, who herself drew a deep breath and was very sympathetic.

"Without doubt," she said brightly, "madame will wish to discuss the nature of the compensation?"

"Something like that," agreed Eve.

"Me, I am of sensibility," said Prue. "Believe me, I am glad madame has shown such gentility in accepting all this. I must confess that for a while there I was worried. I go now; but I shall be upstairs. When you wish to see me, knock on the ceiling with that broomstick, and I descend. *A'voir*, madame. *A'voir*, Tobee."

Gathering up the suspender-belt, the needle, and the thread from the table, Prue made her way towards a door at the back of the sitting room. She gave them a sprightly little sympathetic nod, heightening the prettiness of eyes and lips and teeth, and floated out in a backwash of fleur-de-something, closing the door carefully behind her.

Eve went over and sat down in the easy-chair by the table. She did not say anything.

Toby fidgeted. He walked away from her, putting his elbow on the mantelpiece. The atmosphere of an electrical thunderstorm, gathering in this placid retreat behind the flower shop, could have been felt by a person even more insensitive than Toby Lawes.

To few women has ever been given such an opportunity as was presented to Eve then. After all the aches and bedevilments which had been forced on her, she might have cried aloud that some recompense was only her due. Any fair-minded outsider, seeing those two in the snug room, must have urged her to wade in, with joyous shouts, and smite the enemy hip and thigh. But it is easy for an outsider to say these things.

The silence lengthened. And there was Toby, his elbow on the mantelpiece, twisting at his mustache, hunching his collar up round his ears, and occasionally giving a quick sideways glance at her to see how she was taking it.

Eve said only one word.

"Well?"

XIV

"Look here," Toby blurted out, in his sincere way, "I'm damned sorry about this."

"Are you?"

"I mean, about your learning about it."

"Oh. Aren't you terrified for fear the bank will hear about it too?"

Toby considered this.

"No, that's all right," he assured her. As he stared back at her, a powerful shade of relief went over his face. "Look here, was that what you were worrying about?"

"Perhaps."

"No: I assure you it's perfectly all right," said Toby earnestly. "I'd thought of it, of course. But it's all right so long as you don't involve them in an open scandal. That's the thing: to avoid an open scandal. Otherwise your private life is your own. Just between ourselves,"— he glanced left and right,—"old Dufour, that's the manager, goes to see a poule at Boulogne. Fact! It's well known at the office. I'm telling you that in confidence, naturally."

"Naturally."

Toby's face grew redder yet.

"What I like about you, Eve," he blurted out, "is that you're so damned *understanding*."

"Oh?"

"Yes," said Toby, avoiding her eye. "It isn't a thing we ought to talk about, mind. It isn't a thing I like to talk about to any nice girl, least of all to you. But since the barriers are down . . . well, there you are."

"Yes. The barriers are down, aren't they?"

"Most women would have had conniption fits. I tell you that, straight. You don't know what it's been like these past weeks, even before father died. You may have noticed I haven't been exactly my bright merry self. That little bitch upstairs,"— Eve stiffened, —"I tell you, she's the worst headache I ever had in my life. You can't imagine what I've been through."

"And is that," Eve asked slowly, "is that all you've got to say to me?"

Toby blinked.

"All I've got to say to you?"

Now Eve Neill had been to what are known as the right schools. But at the same time she was still the daughter of old Joe Neill, of Neill's Mills, at Loomhalt in Lancashire. Like old Joe himself, there were certain things she could put up with to an unlimited extent, and other things she could not put up with at all.

As she sat back in Mademoiselle Prue's chair, it seemed to her that she saw the room through a faint mist. She saw the back of Toby's head reflected in the mirror over the mantelpiece, and a tiny bald-spot no bigger than a sixpence amid the woolly hair. The back of that head, somehow, added the last touch to her infuriation.

Eve sat upright.

"*It didn't occur to you,*" she said, "*that you've got a hell of a bloody cheek?*"

In the face of this blast, Toby looked for a second as though he could not believe his ears.

"It didn't occur to you," said Eve, "that there was anything funny in your p-preaching morals at me all day, and acting the high and mighty Sir Galahad, and talking about your ideals and your principles, when all the time you've been keeping this girl on the string ever since you've known me?"

Toby was horrified.

"Really, Eve!" he said. "Really!" And he began to glance quickly and nervously round the room, as though he half expected to find himself face to face with M. Dufour the bank-manager.

"Yes, really!" said Eve. "Blaah!"

"I never expected to hear such language from you."

"Language! What about actions?"

"Well, what about them?" demanded Toby.

"So you can 'forgive and forget' what *I* do, can you? I should jolly well think you could, you — you canting Uriah Heep! And what about your ideals? And you being the simple young man with a pure and holy code?"

Toby was more than perturbed; he was deeply moved with astonishment. He blinked back at her in the same near-sighted way as his mother.

"But that's an altogether different thing," he protested, in a shocked tone like someone explaining something obvious to a child.

"Oh, is it?"

"Yes, it is!"

"How?"

Toby struggled. It was as though he had been asked to expound the interplanetary system, or the construction of the universe, in half a dozen words of one syllable.

"My dear Eve! A man sometimes has . . . well, impulses."

"And do you think a woman doesn't have 'em either?"

"Oh?" snapped Toby. "So you admit it, then?"

"Admit what?"

"That you've started an affair with this swine Atwood after all."

"I never said anything of the kind! I said that a woman ——"

"Oh, no," said Toby, shaking his head like one who has ineffable knowledge above the gods. "Not a nice woman. That's where we differ. If she has, she's not a lady; and she's not worthy of being idealized. That's why I'm so surprised at you, Eve.

"And d'you mind a little more plain speaking, Eve? I wouldn't hurt you for the world. You know that. But I can't, in honesty, help saying what's in my mind. And it seems to me that tonight I'm seeing you in a new light. It seems to me —"

Eve did not interrupt him.

In a detached way she observed that he was standing too close to the fire; that the gray cloth of his suit, behind the calves of the legs, was beginning to scorch and smoke; that in a second more, when he shifted his position, it would sting him like fury. But this prospect failed to upset her.

The interruption was supplied by Mademoiselle Prue, who came flying in after a brief knock, and hurried to the table with an air of nervous apology.

"My — my cotton," she explained. "I seek another spool of cotton." Mademoiselle Prue began to ransack the sewing-basket, while Toby jumped in pain as the cloth scorched his calves, and Eve's soul danced the saraband to watch him.

"Dear Tobee," continued Mademoiselle Prue. "And madame. May I please beg of you not to shout so much? We are respectable here, and it will derange the neighbors."

"Were we shouting?"

"You were shouting very much. I could not understand, because I have no knowledge of English. But it did not seem good." She fished out a spool of red cotton and held it up against the light. "I hope there is no disagreement about this matter of—compensation?"

"Yes," said Eve, there is."

"Madame?"

"I won't buy your lover back from you," said Eve, thereby sending Toby clear up in the air. To do him justice, Toby was as angry over this aspect of the matter as Eve herself.

"But I can make you an offer," continued the . daughter of old Joe Neill. "I will give you double compensation if you persuade your sister Yvette to admit to the police that she locked me out of my house on the night Sir Maurice Lawes was killed."

Prue lost a little of her color, so that the pink-painted lips and dark-lashed eyes stood out with vivid effect.

"I do not know what my sister does!"

"You don't know, for instance, that she is trying

to get me arrested? Presumably in the hope that M. Lawes here will then marry you?"

"Madame!" cried Prue.

(And clearly, Eve thought, she didn't know).

"Don't let that arresting business worry you," growled Toby. "They're bluffing. They don't really mean it?"

"Oh, don't they? They came to my house to take me to jail, half a dozen of them. And I only got away from them by running out and coming here."

Toby tugged at his collar. Though Eve had spoken in English, a very frightened Prue undoubtedly caught the drift of it. She examined another spool of cotton, and threw it on the table.

"The police are coming here?"

"It would not surprise me," retorted Eve.

Prue, with shaking fingers, was grubbing in the sewing-basket and fishing out all manner of articles, which she inspected in a dense way before dropping them on the table. More spools of cotton. A paper of pins. A pair of scissors. Then, in some mysterious fashion, a shoe horn, a rolled tape measure, and a hair-net entangled with a ring.

"Your sister," said Eve, "has a bee in her bonnet. I couldn't have guessed it was you."

"Merci, madame!"

"But it's no good. That cat won't jump. M. Lawes

is not inclined to marry you, as he must have told you himself. On the other hand, I am quite seriously in danger of my life and your sister is in a position to clear me."

"I don't understand what you are talking about. Yvette thinks I am silly. She tells me nothing!"

"Please!" Eve urged desperately. "Your sister must know perfectly well what happened that night. She could tell them that M. Atwood was in my room the whole time. Even if they won't believe him, they may believe her. If the only reason why she wants to get me arrested is this obsession about you, then surely. . ."

Eve checked herself, so startled that she got up from the chair.

Prue had almost gutted the sewing-basket of its contents. Her latest discovery, which she dropped with petulant disdain among the pins and cotton-spools, might have been a piece of cheap costume jewelry. Or it might not. Smallish, square, crystal-like stones, alternating with smallish blue-gleaming stones, were strung together in a thin metal filigree of antique design to form a necklace. As it curled up snakelike where Prue dropped it, the lamplight ran across it with spiteful fires, making the stones wink and sparkle.

"Where," said Eve, "did you get that?"

Prue raised her eyebrows.

"That? It is of no value, madame."

"*No value?*"

"No, madame."

"Diamonds and turquoises." Eve picked it up by one end, so that it curled and swung beside the lamp. "It's Madame de Lamballe's necklace! Unless I've gone completely mad, I last saw this in Papa Lawes's collection. In the curio cabinet immediately to the left of the door as you enter the study."

"Diamonds and turquoises? Madame is mistaken," said Prue, not without bitterness. "Do you doubt that? Well! Let madame go herself to the shop of M. Veille, only a few doors from here, and ask him at what he values it!"

"Yes," interposed Toby in a curious tone. "But where *did* you get it, little one?"

Prue looked from one to the other of them.

"Perhaps I am silly, as my sister says." The self-assured countenance wrinkled up. "Perhaps my idea was not good. Oh, God, if I have made a mistake my sister will kill me! You try to trick me. I do not trust you. I will answer no more questions from either of you. In fact, I — I go to telephone my sister!"

After flinging this out after the fashion of a terrible threat, Prue was out of the room so quickly that they could not have stopped her if they had wished. They heard her sharp, high heels clattering on a staircase behind the door at the back of the shop. Eve dropped the necklace on the table.

"Did you give it to her, Toby?"

"Great Scott, no!"

"Sure?"

"Of course I'm sure. Besides," argued Toby, turning his back abruptly so that he now faced her out of the mirror, "that particular necklace isn't gone!"

"Isn't . . . ?"

"It's still *in* the curio cabinet to the left of the door. At least, it was certainly there when I left our house an hour ago. I remember, Janice called my attention to it."

"Toby," said Eve, "who wore the brown gloves?"

The mirror, a little stained with rust spots, reflected Toby's face oddly.

"When the police were questioning me this afternoon," said Eve, with every nerve in her body strained and fighting, "I didn't tell the whole truth. Ned Atwood *saw* the person who killed your father. I almost saw him.

"Somebody, wearing a pair of brown gloves, went into the study and smashed the snuff-box and killed Papa Lawes. Maybe Ned won't die, you know. And if he doesn't die," — in the mirror, Toby's eyes shifted slightly, —"he'll tell what he saw. *I* can't tell you much, Toby. But I can tell you this much. Whoever did that, it was a member of your own dear, sweet family."

"That's a filthy lie," said Toby, not loudly.

"Is it? You can think so if you like."

"What did your . . . your boy-friend see?"

Eve told him.

"You didn't say anything about this to Goron," Toby pointed out. He seemed to be having difficulty with a dry throat.

"No! And do you know why I didn't?"

"I can't say, I'm sure. Unless it was to cover up your own swooning embraces with —"

"Toby Lawes, do you want me to come over there and slap your face?"

"I see. Growing vulgar, are we?"

"*You* talk about vulgarity?" said Eve.

"I'm sorry." Toby shut his eyes. He clenched his hands on the mantelshelf. "But you don't understand. Eve, this is just about the last straw. I tell you, I won't have my mother or my sister mentioned in connection with this!"

"Who said anything about your mother or your sister? I was only telling you what Ned can testify to, and probably Yvette Latour as well. And I, like a fool, I kept quiet about it because I couldn't bear to hurt you. You were such a noble young man, such a straightforward fellow. . ."

Toby pointed at the ceiling.

"Are you holding *her* against me?" he demanded.

"I'm not holding anything against you."

"Jealous, eh?" asked Toby eagerly.

Eve reflected. "The funny part is that I don't think I am." She started to laugh. "If you could have seen your own face when I walked in here — it might be a good joke if the police weren't a-actually following me, without your doing anything to stop them. And now we find this Mademoiselle Prue with a necklace which looks like. . ."

The portière which closed off the sitting room from the shop in front was made of heavy brown chenille. A hand drew the portière aside. Eve saw the twisted smile — an odd smile, as though the mouth were not quite right — on the face of the tall man in the old sports suit, who removed his hat as he came into the sitting room.

"Excuse me for butting in," observed Dermot Kinross, "but I wonder whether I could have a look at that necklace?"

Toby whirled round.

Dermot went to the table, where he put down his hat. He picked up the string of white and blue stones, and held them under the lamp. He ran them through his fingers. Taking a jeweller's lens from his pocket, he twisted it rather awkwardly into his right eye, and scrutinized the necklace again.

"Yes," he said, with a breath of relief. "That's all right. They're not real."

He dropped the necklace, and returned the lens to his pocket.

Eve found her voice.

"You're with the police! Are they . . . ?"

"Following you? No," smiled Dermot. "As a matter of fact, I came to the rue de la Harpe to see M. Veille the art dealer. I wanted an expert opinion on this."

From his inside pocket he took out an object wrapped in tissue paper. Unwrapping it, and holding it by the end, he displayed a second necklace of shimmering blue and white stones. It was — at first glance — so exactly like the necklace on the table that Eve stared from one to the other of them.

"This," Dermot explained, tapping the exhibit in tissue paper, "is Madame de Lamballe's necklace, from Sir Maurice Lawes's collection. After the crime, you remember, it was found thrown down on the floor under the cabinet?"

"Well?" said Eve.

"I wondered why. These are real diamonds and turquoises." He touched them again. "M. Veille has just assured me of it. But now, it appears, there is a second necklace: a paste imitation. Which, you see, suggests the inference that. . ."

For a moment he remained staring into vacancy. Then he nodded, waking up. Carefully rewrapping the real necklace in its tissue paper, he put it back in his pocket.

"Would you like to tell me," shouted Toby, "just what the hell you're doing here?"

"Am I intruding in your home, sir?"

"You know what I mean. And don't keep politely calling me 'sir'! It sounds as though. . ."

"Yes?"

"As though you're making fun of me!"

Dermot turned to Eve. "I saw you come in. Your taxi-driver assured me you were still here, and the street door was wide open. What I really wanted to tell you was that you're not to worry any longer. The police aren't going to arrest you. Not just yet."

"But they came to my house!"

"Well, they have a habit of doing that. You'll find them in your hair from now on. I can tell you private-ly, though, that one of the persons they wanted to see most was Yvette Latour, who gave them such a great welcome. And if that old virago isn't being given the worst time of her life at this very minute, then I know nothing whatever about French character. . . . Here, steady on!"

"I — I'm all right."

"Have you had any dinner?"

"N-no."

"I thought not. That must be remedied. It's past eleven o'clock, but there are ways of routing out restaurant keepers at any hour. Here's the idea. Our friend Goron has had a slight change of heart, since somebody pointed out to him that a certain member of the Lawes family has been telling a deliberate lie."

At those ominous words "Lawes family," the whole atmosphere changed again. Toby took a step forward.

"Are you in this conspiracy too?"

"There has been a conspiracy, sir. By God, there has! But it wasn't any of my work."

"When you were listening at the door," Toby pointed, emphasizing the fourth word, "did you hear anything? About brown gloves and the rest of it?"

"Yes."

"Didn't it surprise you?"

"No, I can't say it did."

Toby, breathing hard, faced them with an honest appearance of grievance. He fingered the black mourning band on his left sleeve.

"Look here," he said. "I'm not one to air family matters in public, as I think you'll admit. But I ask you, as a reasonable-minded man, whether I haven't been badly let down over this?"

Eve started to speak.

"Wait!" insisted Toby. "I admit — appearances are one thing. But the idea of one of us killing father is such bosh that it looks like a conspiracy. And it came from *her*, mind you!" He pointed. "A woman I trusted, and practically worshipped.

"I told her before that I seemed to be seeing her in a new light. And, by George, I am! She as good as admits she's taken up with this fellow Atwood again. She just couldn't have enough of a bad thing. When I say something to her about it, she flies out and uses language that's not very becoming in the woman I intend to make my wife.

"And why does she talk like that? Because of this girl Prue. Well! I admit it might have been wrong, in a way. But a fellow's got to go out with a little bit of fluff now and then, hasn't he? He doesn't expect to take it seriously. He doesn't expect anybody to take it seriously."

Toby's voice rose.

"That's a very different thing from a woman who pledges her word for marriage. Even if she didn't actually do anything with this swine Atwood, and I'll give her the benefit of the doubt there, still she had him in her room: didn't she? I'm a reputable business man. I can't afford to have people saying my wife did things like that; at least, after it's announced that we're engaged. No: no matter how much I love her. I thought she'd reformed, and I was backing my judgment. But, if this is how she treats me, I'm not sure we oughtn't to consider the engagement at an end."

Honest Toby paused, rather conscience-stricken, for Eve was crying. This was sheer anger and nervous reaction. But Toby did not know it.

"I'm very fond of you, though," he added consolingly.

For about ten seconds, during which the stillness was so absolute that you could hear Mademoiselle Prue herself blubbering upstairs, Dermot Kinross stood without breathing. If he released his breath, he thought it likely that he would explode. Through his mind, itself singed with past pain and humiliation out of which comes wisdom, drifted visions of red murder on his own part.

But he only put his hand with a firm, competent touch on Eve's arm.

"Come out of here," he said gently. "You deserve something better than this."

XV

SUNRISE on the coast of Picardy, in cool September weather, broadens along a horizon as red as the line of a crayon mark; it puts colors in the water, like a drowned paint box; and then, as the sun emerges, little light-points sting the waves of the Channel, blown along by the wind from the Straits of Dover.

On their right was the Channel, on their left scrubby sand-dunes. An asphalt road, following the curve of the shore, itself shone like a river. As the open carriage rattled along it, with a patient coachman on the box and two passengers behind him, each creak and jingle of harness, each clop of horse's hoofs, seemed to have a separate brittle noise against the light-headed hush and emptiness of morning.

The breeze from the Channel blew Eve's hair wildly, and made ripples in the dark fur of her coat. Yet, despite the hollows under her eyes, she was laughing.

"Do you realize," she cried, "that you've kept me talking all night?"

"That's all right," said Dermot.

The top-hatted coachman did not turn round or say anything. But his shoulders hunched up almost to his ears.

"And where are we, anyway?" said Eve. "We must be five or six miles from La Bandelette!"

Once more the coachman's shoulders expressed agreement.

"That doesn't matter," Dermot assured her. "Now, about this story of yours."

"Yes?"

"I want you to tell it to me again. Every word of it."

"AGAIN?"

This time the coachman's shoulders rose above the level of his ears, a contortionistic feat possible only to those of his tribe. He cracked his whip and the carriage spanked along, bouncing its occupants as they tried to look at each other.

"Please," said Eve. "I've told it to you four times. I haven't left out one single detail, I swear, of what happened — well, on that night. My voice is a croak. I must look a sight." She held back her hair with both hands. The gray eyes, stung with moisture from the wind, implored him. "Couldn't we at least put it off until after breakfast?"

Dermot was jubilant.

He leaned back against the faded upholstery of the seat, flexing his shoulders. He was somewhat light-headed from lack of sleep, and from a certain discovery which made his wits turn round to look where they had not looked too closely before. He had forgotten the fact that he needed a shave and looked thoroughly disreputable. It was a mighty surge of elation: he felt that he could have picked up the whole world, and balanced it, and chucked it downstairs.

"Well, maybe we can spare you," he conceded. "After all, I think I've got the main details. You see, Mrs. Neill, you've told me something very important."

"What's that?"

"You've told me who the murderer is," said Dermot.

While the rattletrap seemed to fly, Eve leaned out and steadied herself against the support over which the carriage rug was folded.

"But *I* haven't got the least idea!" she protested.

"I know. That's why your account is so valuable. If you did know what had happened —"

He glanced at her sideways, hesitating.

"I had an idea, just a ghost of an idea, yesterday," he went on, "that I might be looking in the wrong direction. But I never woke up fully until you started telling your story over the omelettes at Papa Rousse's last night."

"Dr. Kinross," said Eve, "which one of them did it?"

"Does it matter to you? Does it make any difference," he touched his chest, "here?"

"No. But — which one of them did it?"

Dermot looked her in the eyes.

"I am, quite deliberately, not going to tell you."

Eve felt that she had had quite enough of this. But, as she opened her mouth for angry protest, she caught the steady, heartening friendliness of his look: the power of sympathy which had almost the power to burn.

"Listen," he went on. "I'm not saying that like the great detective, in order to astonish the weak-minded in the last chapter. I'm saying it for the very best reason a psychologist can have. The secret of this matter," — he reached out to touch her forehead, — "is here. In your brain."

"But I still don't understand!"

"You know it. But you're not aware that you know it. If I told you, you would start to think back. You would supply interpretations. You would rearrange facts. And that mustn't happen. Not yet. Everything — do you hear? *everything* — depends on your telling that story to Goron and the examining magistrate exactly as you told it to me."

Eve moved uneasily.

"Let me give you an illustration," suggested Dermot, studying her. He fished in his waistcoat pocket, and took out his watch. He held it up. "For instance, what's this?"

"I beg your pardon?"

"What's this I've got in my hand?"

"It's a watch, Mr. Conjuror."

"How do you know that? There's a strong wind blowing. You can't hear it tick."

"But, my dear man, I can *see* it's a watch!"

"Exactly. That's what I meant. We also observe by the watch," he added more lightly, "that it's twenty minutes past five o'clock, and you are very definitely in need of sleep. — Coachman!"

"Yes, monsieur?"

"Better get back to the town."

"YES, MONSIEUR!"

You might have thought that the patient driver had been touched by magic. The effect of his swinging the carriage round was like one of those news-reel effects by which the film is speeded up, and a whole street suddenly becomes galvanized. They were rattling back along the same road, with white gulls squawking above a gray-blue Channel, when Eve spoke again.

"And now?"

"Sleep. Afterwards, trust your obedient servant. You'll have to see Goron and the examining magistrate today."

"Yes. I suppose so."

"This M. Vautour, the examining magistrate, has the reputation of being a terror. But don't be afraid of him. If he stands on his rights, as he may, they probably won't allow me to be present at the interview . . ."

"You won't be there?" cried Eve.

"I'm not a lawyer, you see. You'd better have a lawyer, by the way. I'll send Saulomon round to you." He paused. "Does it make so much difference," he added, looking hard at the coachman's back, "whether I'm there or not?"

"It does, rather. I haven't thanked you for . . ."

"Oh, that's all right. As I was saying, just tell your story, *in detail*, mind, as you told it to me. As soon as that story is officially in the record, I can act."

"What are you going to do in the meantime?"

Dermot was silent for a long while.

"There's one person who can testify who the murderer is," he replied. "That's Ned Atwood. But he's no good to us yet, though I'm staying at the Donjon Hotel too and I'll look in on his doctor just on the off-chance. No." Again he paused. "I'm going to London."

Eve sat up. "To London?"

"Only for the day. There's a ten-thirty plane from here, and a late afternoon one from Croydon which should get me back by dinner time. I ought to have definite news by that time, if my plan of campaign works out."

"Dr. Kinross, why are you taking all this trouble for me?"

"Oh, we can't have a fellow countryman in danger of being chucked into the cooler. Now can we?"

"Don't joke!"

"Was I joking? I'm sorry."

His flick of a smile contradicted the apology. Eve's eyes searched his face. Conscious of something in harsh sunlight, Dermot suddenly put up a hand to his cheek as though to hide it; the old phobia returned and stabbed. Eve did not notice. In her present tired state, shivering under the short fur wrap, she found the events of the past night looming large in her mind.

"I must have bored you terribly," she said, "with all that talk about my love-life."

"You know you didn't."

"I simply poured out confessions, to a perfect stranger, until I'm half ashamed to look you in the face now that it's daylight again."

"Why not? That's what I was there for. But may I ask a question — for the first time?"

"Of course."

"What are you going to do about Toby Lawes?"

"What would *you* do, if you'd been handed the mitten in that suave and gracious way? I was properly jilted, wasn't I? And in front of a witness too."

"Do you think you're still in love with him? I don't ask if you are. I only ask if you think you are."

Eve did not reply. The hoofs of the horse rang with a hard, clear clatter on the road. Presently Eve laughed.

"I don't seem to have much luck with my men, do I?"

She said no more, and Dermot did not pursue the matter. It was nearly six o'clock when they clattered back into the white, swept streets of La Bandelette, where nothing stirred except a few early-morning hearties out on horseback. Eve's teeth fastened in her lower lip, and she grew a shade paler, as the carriage swung into the rue des Anges. Dermot assisted her out of the carriage in front of her own villa.

Eve cast a quick glance at the Villa Bonheur across the street. It seemed blank and drained of life, except for one upstairs bedroom window. The shutters on this window were folded back. Helena Lawes, wearing an Oriental kimono, her eyeglasses on her nose, was standing there motionless, looking at them.

Their voices sounded so loud in the hushed street that Eve instinctively whispered.

"L-look behind you. Did you notice the upstairs window?"

"Yes."

"Shall I take any notice?"

"No."

Eve's expression grew desperate. "Couldn't you *possibly* tell me who . . . ?"

"No. I'll tell you only one thing. You were deliberately chosen to be the victim in as careful and cruel and cold-blooded a little scheme as I've come across. The person who planned it deserves no mercy, and is going to get none. I shall see you tonight. And then, heaven willing, we are going to settle somebody's hash."

"Anyway," said Eve, "thanks. Thanks, thanks, thanks!"

She pressed his hand, opened the gate, and ran up the path to the front door, while the coachman uttered a weary sigh of relief; and Dermot, after standing for so long on the pavement staring at her house that the driver had new apprehensions, climbed back into the carriage.

"Donjon Hotel, *mon gars*. Then your labors will be finished."

At the hotel he paid his cab-fare, added an enormous tip, and went up the steps followed by an epic torrent of thanks. The Donjon, whose foyer attempts to reproduce the hall of a mediaeval castle, was just waking up.

Dermot went to his room. From his pocket he took the diamond and turquoise necklace, borrowed from M. Goron; he made it into a registered packet, to be sent back to the prefect, and enclosed a note explaining he must be away for the day. Then he shaved, took a cold shower to clear his head, and ordered up breakfast while he dressed.

The reception clerk informed him by phone that the number of M. Atwood's room was 401. After breakfast Dermot went to find it, and was fortunate enough to meet the hotel physician, on his early-morning round, just leaving Ned's bedside.

Dr. Boutet was much impressed at the sight of Dermot's professional card. But he betrayed a certain impatience. He stood in the dim-lit corridor outside the bedroom, and expressed himself forcibly.

"No, monsieur, M. Atwood is *not* conscious. Twenty times a day someone comes from the prefecture of police, and asks the same question."

"There is, naturally, no telling if he will ever be so. On the other hand, it might occur at any minute?"

"That is possible, from the nature of the injury. I will show you the X-rays."

"I should be grateful. Has he, do you think, a chance?"

"In my opinion, yes."

"Has he said anything? In his delirium, perhaps?"

"He laughs sometimes. But that is all. In any case, I am not often with him. It would be necessary to put that question to the nurse."

"May I see him?"

"But of course!"

In a darkened room, overlooking the rich flower gardens behind the hotel, the man who knew the secret lay like a corpse. The nurse was a Sister of some religious order; her huge headdress loomed in silhouette against the dim white blinds.

Dermot studied the sick man. A handsome devil, he thought bitterly. Eve Neill's first love, and perhaps . . . he put that thought away from him. If Eve were still in love with the fellow, even subconsciously, there was nothing he could do about it. He took Ned's pulse, and the ticking of his watch animated the quiet. Dr. Boutet showed him the X-ray photographs, speaking with relish of the miracle by which his patient had lived as long as this.

"Say anything, monsieur?" repeated the nurse, in reply to Dermot's question. "Yes, he mutters sometimes."

"Well?"

"But he speaks in English. I do not understand

English. And then, very often, he laughs and calls out a name."

Dermot, who had been turning towards the door, whirled round again.

"*What name?*"

"Sh-h!" admonished Dr. Boutet.

"I cannot say, monsieur. All the syllables sound alike. No, monsieur, I regret that I cannot give you an imitation." The nurse's eyes were anxious in the gloom. "If you insist, I will try to write down what it sounds like when he says it again."

No: there was nothing more here. Dermot had done what he came to do. He had a few more inquiries to make, in the various bars of the hotel, where one waiter spoke with enthusiasm of little Mees Janice Lawes. Sir Maurice himself, it appeared, had looked into the noisy back bar on the very afternoon before his death: surprising barman and waiters.

"How he has ferocious eyes!" rumbled the barman. "Afterwards Jules Seznec sees him walking in the Zoological Gardens, beside the monkey house, talking to someone whom Jules cannot see because the other person is hidden behind a bush."

Then Dermot had just time to telephone Maître Saulomon, his legal friend of the firm of Saulomon & Cohen, before he booked a seat in the Imperial Airways plane leaving La Bandelette airport at half-past ten.

The rest of the day he afterwards remembered as something of a nightmare. In the plane he dozed, to recuperate himself for the important part of the journey. The bus trip from Croydon seemed interminable; and London, after some days of rest, seemed choked with soot and petrol fumes. Dermot took a taxi to a certain address. Half an hour later, he could have shouted for triumph.

He had proved what he came to prove. When, under a yellow evening sky, he climbed into the plane which was to take him back to La Bandelette, he felt tired no longer. The engines thundered; wind-rush blew flat the grass as the plane taxied in a bump of balloon tires; and Eve was safe. Dermot, his briefcase in his lap, sat back in his seat while air ventilators buzzed in the stuffy cabin, watching England dwindle first to red-and-gray roofs, and then to a moving map.

Eve was safe. And Dermot made plans. He was still making them, just before dark, when the plane dipped down at the airport. A few lights twinkled in the direction of the town. Driving back through the avenue of close-set trees, breathing the clean pine-scented air at dusk, Dermot let his mind run beyond the present bedevilment to a future when...

An orchestra was playing at the Donjon Hotel. The lights and clamor of the foyer struck against his senses. As he·passed the reception desk, a clerk signalled him.

"Docteur Kinross! There have been inquiries for you all day. One moment! I believe there are two persons waiting to see you even now."

"Who are they?"

"A Monsieur Saulomon," replied the clerk, consulting a pad, "and a Mademoiselle Lawes."

"Where are they?"

"Somewhere in the foyer, monsieur." The clerk struck on a bell. "I will have you taken to them. Yes?"

Escorted by a page-boy, Dermot found Janice Lawes and Maître Pierre Saulomon in one of the alcoves of the alleged "Gothic" foyer. The alcove had sham stone walls, and was hung with sham mediaeval weapons. A padded seat ran round it, with a little table in the middle. Janice and Maître Saulomon sat very far apart, as though each brooded over a separate trouble. But both of them got up as Dermot approached; and he was astounded to see the look of reproach on their faces.

Maître Saulomon was a very large fat man with an imposing manner, an olive complexion, and a deep bass voice. He gave Dermot a very curious look.

"So you have returned, my friend," he stated in that sepulchral voice.

"Naturally! I told you to expect me. Where is Mrs. Neill?"

The lawyer inspected the finger nails of one hand, turning them from side to side. Then he looked up.

"She is at the town hall, my friend."

"At the town hall? Still? They're keeping her there a long time, aren't they?"

Maître Saulomon's expression became grim.

"She is locked up in a cell," he answered. "And I much fear, old man, that she will be kept there an even longer time. Madame Neill has been placed under arrest on a charge of murder."

XVI

"Tell me, my boy," pursued the imposing personage, in a tone of real interest. "Just in confidence. And between friends. Are you mocking me?"

"Or mocking *her*?" interposed Janice.

Dermot stared at them.

"I don't quite understand what you're talking about."

Maître Saulomon pointed a finger at him, waggling it as though asking a question in court.

"Did you, or did you not," he said, "instruct Madame Neill to tell her story to the police, in every detail, exactly as she seems to have told it to you?"

"Yes, of course I did!"

"Ah!" rumbled Maître Saulomon, with rich satisfaction. He squared himself, putting two fingers into his waistcoat pocket. "My friend, have you gone out of your mind? Are you stark, staring mad?"

"Look here . . ."

"Up to this afternoon, when they questioned Madame Neill, the police are almost convinced of her innocence. Almost! You have made them waver."

"Well?"

"But — the moment she finishes her testimony — they waver no longer. M. Goron and the examining magistrate look at each other. Madame Neill has made a slip so fatal, so damning to anyone who knows the evidence, that there can be no doubt of her guilt. Boum! It is finished. All my skill, even mine, could do nothing for her."

On the little table, beside Janice Lawes, there was a half-empty Martini and three stacked saucers to indicate three previous drinks. Janice sat down and finished the Martini, accentuating the slight flush on her face. If Helena had been there, Helena would have said many things. But Dermot was not concerned with this aspect of the girl's character.

He stared back at Maître Saulomon.

"One moment!" he urged. "Had this so-called 'slip' of hers something to do with — the Emperor's snuff-box?"

"It had."

"Her description of it, I mean?"

"Exactly."

Dermot dropped his brief-case on the table.

"Well, well!" he said, with a full-blown and sardonic bitterness which made the others draw back. "Then the very evidence which should have convinced them she's innocent is the very evidence which convinces them she's guilty?"

The lawyer shrugged his elephantine shoulders.

"I can't say what you mean by that."

"M. Goron," said Dermot, "gives the impression of being an intelligent man. What in God's name has gone wrong with him?" He brooded. "Or gone wrong with her, maybe?"

"She was certainly upset," the lawyer admitted. "Her story was not altogether impressive even on the points which might reasonably be called truth."

"I see. Then she *didn't* give the account to Goron as she gave it to me this morning?"

Again Maître Saulomon shrugged his shoulders.

"As to what she may have told you, that's another pair of sleeves. I can't say."

"May I have a word?" interposed Janice softly.

Janice twirled the stem of the cocktail glass. After several false starts, she spoke to Dermot in English.

"I don't know what's going on. I've been tagging about all day after Appius Claudius here," — she nodded towards Maître Saulomon, — "and all he'll do is make noises in his throat and stand on his dignity. We're all a good deal on edge. Mother and Toby and Uncle Ben are at the town hall now."

"Oh? Are they?"

"Yes. Trying to see Eve. And failing conspicuously." Janice hesitated. "I gathered from Toby that there was a royal dust-up last night. It seems Toby wasn't in his right mind (he often isn't), and said some things to Eve he's regretting horribly today. I never saw the poor boy so conscience-stricken."

After a quick glance at Dermot's face, which had grown grim enough to mark a danger sign, Janice continued to twirl the stem of the cocktail glass in even more unsteady fingers.

"These last couple of days," she continued, "everything hasn't been exactly gas and gaiters. But we *are* on Eve's side, in spite of what you may think. When we heard about her arrest, we were as thunderstruck as you."

"I am gratified to hear it."

"Please don't talk like that! You look like — an executioner, or something."

"Thank you. I hope to be one."

Janice looked up quickly. "Of whom?"

"When I last spoke to Goron," said Dermot, ignoring the question, "he had two good cards to play for all they were worth. One was what is known as a grilling of Yvette Latour, from which he expected results. The other was the fact that a certain person, in describing events on the night of the murder, has been telling lies. Why the devil he's thrown those cards into the dust-bin in order to arrest Eve is beyond what feeble wits I can bring into this business."

"You might ask him," suggested the lawyer, nodding towards the foyer. "He is coming to join us now."

Aristide Goron, as bland and dapper as ever despite a worried forehead, made a great play of striking the ferrule of his stick on the floor as he stumped towards them; he had a walk like the Grand Monarch.

"Ah! Good evening, my friend," he greeted Dermot, with a faintly defensive note in his voice. "You have returned from London, I see."

"Yes. To find a beautiful situation here."

"One regrets," sighed M. Goron. "Still, justice is justice. You acknowledge that? May one further ask why it was necessary for you to rush to London like that?"

"In order," answered Dermot, "to get proof of motive against the real murderer of Sir Maurice Lawes."

"Ah, zut!" exploded M. Goron.

Dermot turned to Maître Saulomon. "It will be necessary for me to have a little conversation with the prefect of police. Miss Lawes, will you excuse my discourtesy if I ask to have a word with these gentlemen in private?"

Janice rose with the utmost composure.

"Shall I make myself scarce, or what?"

"Not at all. M. Saulomon will join you in a moment, and take you back to your family at the town hall."

He waited until Janice — whether angry or merely

mocking could not be told — had gone out of the alcove. Then he addressed the lawyer.

"Could you, my friend, manage to convey a message to Eve Neill?"

"I can at least try," shrugged Maître Saulomon.

"Good. You might tell her that, after I have spoken to M. Goron, I hope to effect her release within an hour or two at the outside. For good measure, I propose to hand over the real murderer of Sir Maurice Lawes in her place."

There was a pause.

"This is hokey-pokey!" cried M. Goron, shaking the malacca stick in the air. "This is a juggle with words. I tell you, I will have nothing to do with it!"

But the lawyer bowed. He moved out into the foyer, like a galleon under full sail. They saw him stop to address a word to Janice. He offered his arm, which she refused. Yet they left the foyer together, disappearing into the throng. Then Dermot, seating himself on the bench in the alcove, opened his briefcase.

"Will you sit down, M. Goron?"

The prefect swelled. "No, monsieur, I will NOT sit down!"

"Oh, come! Considering what I can promise you—"

"Pfaa!"

"Why not be comfortable and take something to drink?"

"Well!" growled M. Goron, still on his dignity but relaxing nevertheless. He sat down on the padded seat. "Perhaps a little moment. And perhaps a small glass of something to drink. If monsieur insists, I will have a hokey-pokey . . . I mean, I will have a visky-soda."

Dermot ordered the drinks.

"You surprise me," he said with ferocious suavity. "After such a sensational capture as arresting Madame Neill, why aren't you at the town hall pounding her with questions?"

"I have business at this hotel," replied M. Goron, and drummed his fingers on the table.

"Business?"

"In effect," said M. Goron, moving his neck. "Some while ago Dr. Boutet telephones me. He says that M. Atwood has recovered consciousness, and that perhaps some small judicious questioning might be permitted. . ."

At the expression of satisfaction on Dermot's face, the prefect simmered again.

"Then I tell you this," Dermot said. "M. Atwood is going to tell you exactly what I am going to tell you. That will be the last link. If he confirms what I say, without any prompting from me, will you give my evidence a hearing?"

"Evidence? What evidence?"

"One moment," interrupted Dermot. "Why have you done this about-face turn and arrested the lady?"

M. Goron told him.

The prefect explained with a wealth of detail, punctuated by sips from a visky-soda. Though M. Goron did not seem altogether happy even now, Dermot had to admit that there was some cloud of reason in the prefect's suspicions and the thunderous certainty of M. Vautour the examining magistrate.

"Then," muttered Dermot, "she didn't tell you after all. She didn't tell you what slipped out, when she was half dead from lack of sleep this morning. She didn't tell you the one really important thing which completes her defence and proves the case against somebody else."

"Which is?"

"Listen!" said Dermot, and opened the brief-case on the table.

When he began to speak, the hands of the ornate clock in the foyer stood at five minutes to nine. By five minutes past, M. Goron had begun to squirm and hunch his shoulders. By fifteen minutes past, the prefect had become silent: quiet and worried, turning up his palms in a way which indicated supplication.

"I detest this affair," he groaned. "I abominate this affair. No sooner are you right-side-up, than along comes somebody and turns you down-side-up again."

"Does it explain everything that's seemed so difficult before?"

"This time, I make no reply! I am cautious. But, in effect . . . yes, it does."

"Then the case is complete. You have only to ask that one question from the man who saw what happened. Ask Ned Atwood, '*Was it so-and-so?*' If he says yes, you can prepare your violin to good purpose. And you can't accuse me of having prompted him."

M. Goron rose to his feet, finishing the visky-soda.

"Let us go and have our throats cut," he invited.

For the second time that day Dermot visited room 401. But on the previous occasion he had not expected such a stroke of luck as greeted him now. It was as though two influences, one good and the other ironically malign, carried Eve Neill's destiny between them and were always tripping each other up.

A dim lamp burned in the bedroom. Ned Atwood, though very pale and somewhat blurred of eye, was very much awake. Trying to sit up weakly, he was expostulating with the night nurse, a stout and cheery West Country girl from the English Hospital, who appeared engaged in an attempt to hold him down.

"Sorry to disturb you," Dermot began. "But —"

"Look," said Ned, in a husky croak which made him clear his throat several times. He peered past the nurse's arm. "Are you the doctor? Then for God's sake get this harpy off me, will you? She's been trying to sneak up and stick me with a hypodermic."

"Lie down," fumed the nurse. "You've got to be *quiet*!"

"How the hell can I be quiet when you won't tell me what's happened? I don't want to be quiet. That's the last thing in the world I do want. I promise to be good; I promise to take every filthy medicine in the codex; if you'll just have the common decency to tell me what happened."

"It's all right, nurse," Dermot said, as the girl regarded them suspiciously.

"May I ask who you are, sir? And what you're doing here?"

"I am Dr. Kinross. This is M. Goron, the prefect of police, who is investigating the murder of Sir Maurice Lawes."

As though a blurred lens had come into focus, the expression on Ned Atwood's face slowly sharpened; comprehension came back into it. Breathing thinly, he half sat up, supporting himself with his hands behind his back. He peered down at his pajamas, as though he had never seen them before. He blinked at corners of the room.

"I was coming up in the lift," he announced, with careful articulation, "when all of a sudden I . . ." He touched his throat. "How long have I been like this?"

"Nine days."

"*Nine days?*"

"That's right. Were you really struck by a car outside the hotel, Mr. Atwood?"

"Car? What damn nonsense is this about a car?"

"You said you were."

"I never said anything of the kind. At least, I don't remember saying anything like that." Full comprehension now returned. "*Eve*," he said, expressing everything in one word.

"Yes. Will you try not to get excited, Mr. Atwood, if I tell you that she's in trouble and needs your help?"

"Do you want to kill him?" demanded the nurse.

"Shut up," ordered Ned, with conspicuous lack of gallantry. "Trouble?" he asked Dermot. "What do you mean by trouble?"

It was the prefect of police who answered. M. Goron, his arms folded, attempted to remain self-effacing and to betray nothing of the rather complicated emotions which obsessed him then.

"Madame is in prison," the prefect of police said in English. "She has been charged with murdering Sir Maurice Lawes."

During the long pause which followed, a cool night breeze stirred the curtains and the white blinds at the windows. Ned, now propped bolt upright, stared back at them. His white pajama coat was rucked up round his shoulders; his arms showed thin and white after nine days of losing weight. They had shaved the crown of his head, as is customary in such cases. Its thin gauze plastering made an almost ludicrous contrast to the white, gaunt, handsome face with the washed-out blue eyes and reckless mouth. All of a sudden he started to laugh.

"Is this a joke?"

"No," Dermot assured him. "The evidence is very strong against her. And the Lawes family are doing very little to help."

"I'll bet they are," said Ned. He threw back the bed-clothes, and started to climb out of bed.

The ensuing moments were chaotic.

"Now, look!" said Ned, tottering on his feet but clinging firmly with one hand to the table beside the bed. The old grinning animation was back in his expression. He seemed convulsed by some huge inner amusement, a joke whispered to the reeds and too deep to share.

"I'm supposed to be a sick man," he went on, as a wheel seemed to go round behind his eyes. "Right! Then humor me. I want my clothes. What for? To go to the town hall, of course. If I don't get 'em, I'm going to go over and hop out that window; and Eve herself could tell you I mean every blasted word I say."

"Mr. Atwood," said the nurse, "if I ring for someone to hold you down. . . ."

"And I say unto you, sweetie, that I could be out of that window before your fair hand touched the bell. At the moment all I can see is a hat. I'll make my dive in that if necessary."

He appealed to Dermot and M. Goron.

"I don't know what's been happening in this town since I passed out. You can inform me, if you will, while we're on the way to see Eve. You see, gentlemen, there are wheels within wheels in this business. You don't understand."

"I think we do," answered Dermot. "Mrs. Neill has told us about the person in the brown gloves."

"But I bet she hasn't told you who it was. Because why? Because she doesn't know."

"And *you* know?" inquired M. Goron.

"Of course," returned Ned, at which M. Goron removed his bowler hat with every serious indication of an intent to drive his fist through it. Ned remained teetering and grinning by the table, his forehead furrowed with horizontal wrinkles. "She's told you, maybe, about our looking across there and seeing somebody with the old man? And then, afterwards, seeing him when he'd been hit? But that's the point. That's the whole joke. It was. . . ."

XVII

"MESDAMES and messieurs," bowed M. Vautour the examining magistrate, "please enter my humble office."

"Thanks," murmured Janice.

"Is this where you're going to let us speak to poor Eve?" panted Helena. "How is the dear girl taking it, by the way?"

"Not too well, I should imagine," volunteered Uncle Ben.

Toby said nothing. He had thrust his hands deep into his pockets, and shook his head in moody sympathy.

The town hall at La Bandelette is a tall, narrow, yellow-stone building with a clock tower, facing a pleasant park and not far from the Central Market. The office of M. Vautour, a big room on the top floor, had two wide windows facing north and another facing west. There were filing cabinets, a few dusty-looking legal books — the examining magistrate must be a lawyer — and a framed photograph of some forgotten dignitary in Legion-of-Honor uniform.

M. Vautour's desk was so placed that M. Vautour had his back to the west window when he sat there.

A little way out from the desk, facing him, stood a worn wooden armchair. A hanging light was suspended over this chair.

Then the visitors noticed something else: something, it seemed to them, at once childish and terrifying.

Through the uncurtained west window leaped a dazzle of blinding white light, paralyzing the eyes. It made them jump. It swept one side of the room, like a white broom that scrapes skin, seemed to burst after the fashion of a bubble, and disappear. It was the beam of the great lighthouse. A person sitting in the witness chair — facing M. Vautour's desk — would have that blinding glare rake across his eyes, once every twenty seconds, as certain and impersonal as fate, so long as the examining magistrate kept him sitting there.

"Ah, that annoying lighthouse!" murmured M. Vautour, dismissing it with a wave of his hand. He indicated chairs on the side of the room where the beam did not fall. "Please sit down, and make yourselves comfortable."

M. Vautour sat down behind his desk, swivelling the chair sideways to face them.

The examining magistrate was a bony elderly man, with a hard eye and a suspicion of side-whisker. He rubbed his hands together with a dry noise.

"Are we going to see Mrs. Neill?" demanded Toby.

"Well ... no," replied M. Vautour. "Not just yet."

"And why not?"

"Because I think, first of all, that there are some explanations due to me."

Again the white blaze dazzled at the window, pouring past M. Vautour's shoulder. It turned him into a silhouette, despite the ceiling light; it kindled the edge of his gray hair, and showed him rubbing his hands again. Otherwise nothing could have been homelier than the lair of this theatrical gentleman. A clock ticked, and the office cat was curled up on a side table.

Yet they could almost feel wrath flowing from the direction of the examining magistrate.

"I have just had," he pursued, "a lengthy conversation on the telephone with my colleague M. Goron. He is at the Donjon Hotel. He spoke of new evidence. He will be here at any minute, with his friend Dr. Kinross."

Here M. Vautour struck the desk with the palm of his hand.

"I do not necessarily admit," he said, "that we were precipitate. I do not necessarily admit, even now, that we were too hasty in arresting Madame Neill. . . ."

"Wow!" exclaimed Toby.

"But this new evidence is startling. It upsets me. It makes me return to a certain point, indicated some time ago by Dr. Kinross, which in our natural concern with Madame Neill we were almost in danger of forgetting."

"Toby," Helena asked quietly, "what did happen last night?"

Turning, she stretched out her hand towards M. Vautour across the room. Helena was now perhaps the coolest of the Lawes family, all of whom seemed to sense a trap.

"M. Vautour," Helena pursued, getting her breath, "let me tell you. Last night my son came home late. He came in storming. . . ."

"That," Toby interrupted in desperation, "hasn't got anything to do with father's death!"

"I was still up, because I couldn't sleep, and I asked him if he would have a cup of cocoa. He went banging up to his bedroom without exchanging three words." Helena's face clouded. "All I could gather was that he had had a dreadful quarrel of some kind with Eve, whom he said he never wanted to see again."

M. Vautour rubbed his hands together. Again the white glare flared across his shoulder.

"Ah!" murmured the examining magistrate. "And

did he tell you where he had been, madame?"

Helena looked puzzled. "No. Should he have told me?"

"Number 17, rue de la Harpe? He did not mention that?"

Helena shook her head.

Both Janice and Uncle Ben were watching Toby. A close observer might have seen that a brief, crooked smile flashed across Janice's face, to be veiled demurely by the gravity of a young lady who has taken four cocktails on an empty stomach. Uncle Ben was scraping the inside of an empty pipe with a pocket-knife; the small rasps of the knife seemed badly to afflict Toby's nerves. But Helena, who evidently noticed nothing, was continuing in the same pleading tone.

"A quarrel with Eve seemed to me just about the last straw. I couldn't sleep at all for thinking of it. In fact, I saw her come home well after daylight with that rather sinister-looking man who's supposed to be a great doctor. On top of *that*, Eve is arrested. Are any of these things connected? Could you possibly tell us what's happening?"

"Second the motion," observed Uncle Ben.

M. Vautour's jaws tightened.

"Then your son has told you nothing at all, madame?"

"I've said so."

"Not even, for instance, of Madame Neill's accusation?"

"Accusation?"

"That some member of your family, wearing a pair of brown gloves, crept into Sir Maurice's study and beat the old man to death."

There was a long silence. Toby, sitting forward in his chair, put his head in his hands; he kept shaking his head violently, as though this were the one suggestion he could not countenance.

"I knew those brown gloves were going to pop up somehow," remarked Uncle Ben, in a startlingly normal tone. He seemed to inspect the idea from all sides. "You mean the girl . . . saw something?"

"And if she did, M. Phillips?"

Uncle Ben smiled a dry smile. "If she did, my friend, you wouldn't be suggesting. You'd be arresting. So I think we can take it that she didn't. Murder in the family, eh? Well, well, well!"

"It's no good saying," Janice blurted out, "that the same idea hasn't occurred to all of us."

Helena eyed her in evident stupefaction.

"It certainly hasn't to me! My dear Janice! Have you gone out of your mind? Have we all gone out of our minds?"

"See here," began Uncle Ben, and drew at the empty pipe.

He waited for them to give him a glance of forebearing tolerance, such as usually greeted a suggestion of his which did not deal with the practical mechanics of a household. There was a frown on his face, and a mild doggedness in his manner.

"It's no good making ourselves out as stupider than we are. Of course it's occurred to all of us. God damn it all!" The others straightened up, shocked at the change in his tone. "Let's stop being such a 'civilized' family. Let's let air and daylight into our souls . . . if we've got any."

"Ben!" cried Helena.

"That house was locked up. Doors and windows. It wasn't a burglar. You don't have to be a detective to guess that. Either Eve Neill did it, or one of us did."

"And do you think," demanded Helena, "that I'd put the welfare of a total stranger before the welfare of one of my own flesh and blood?"

"Well, then," said Uncle Ben patiently, "why be a hypocrite? Why not come out and *say* you believe she did it?"

Helena was flustered.

"Because I'm very fond of the girl. And she has got quite a lot of money, which can be very useful to

Toby. Or could have been, if I could only get away from the idea that she might have done that to Maurice. But I can't get away from it, and it's no good saying I can."

"Then you believe Eve is guilty?"

"I don't know!" wailed Helena.

"Perhaps," observed M. Vautour in a cold, hard, steady voice which instantly quieted them, "we can have a little elucidation soon. —— Come in!"

The door to the hall outside was directly opposite the west window. With each revolution the search-light-beam wheeled up across this door, throwing on the pale-glowing panels a pattern from the dust of the window. Someone had knocked at this door. In response to M. Vautour's command, Dermot Kinross came in.

The glare was just wheeling past as he entered. Though Dermot lifted a hand to shield his eyes, they saw in its passionless clearness a face of controlled wrath: a dangerous face, changing as soon as he knew he was observed to the easy-going suavity which was his public mood. He bowed to them. Going across to the examining magistrate, he shook hands in the formal French fashion.

M. Vautour had none of M. Goron's blandness.

"I have not seen you, monsieur," he said coldly, "since our first introduction last night, before you departed for the rue de la Harpe with that very interesting necklace."

"A good deal," said Dermot, "has happened since then."

"So I understand. This new evidence of yours — well, there may be something in it! In any case, there is your party." He waved his hand towards the others. "Attack! Stick them in the gizzard, faith! Then we shall see what we shall see."

"M. Goron," continued Dermot, looking sideways at the visitors, "is bringing Madame Neill upstairs to this office. You will allow that?"

"Of course, of course!"

"And, speaking of the question of necklaces, M. Goron says you have both of them here."

The examining magistrate nodded. Opening a drawer of his desk, he drew out two objects which he laid on the blotter. As the white light wheeled again, it stirred to life two lines of fiery points which ran across the blotter. A diamond-and-turquoise necklace, and an imitation which at first glance might have been mistaken for the first necklace, lay side by side. To the second necklace was attached a small card.

"According to the note you wrote to M. Goron," the examining magistrate told him sourly, "we sent a man to the rue de la Harpe, claimed the imitation, and traced it. You observe?"

He touched the card. Dermot nodded.

"Though I am only now beginning to perceive the meaning of this," snapped M. Vautour. "Today (I assure you!) we were much too busy with Madame Neill and the snuff-box to trouble our heads about anyone else and these necklace-twins."

Dermot turned round, and went towards the quiet group across the room.

They resented him. He could feel the force of that resentment, all the more bitter for being unspoken; in a way, it pleased him. While M. Vautour sat spiderlike in the background, and the searchlight flicked its white surge across the wall, Dermot drew out a chair. Its legs rasped on the linoleum of the floor as he set it round to face them.

"Yes," he acknowledged in English. "As you were thinking, I'm butting in."

"Why?" asked Uncle Ben.

"Because somebody's got to, or this mess will never be straightened out. Have you heard about the famous brown gloves? Good! Then let me tell you a little more about them."

"Including," said Janice, "who wore them?"

"Yes," said Dermot.

He sat back in the chair, thrusting his hands into his pockets.

"I want to call your attention," he went on, "to

the afternoon, evening, and night of the day when Sir Maurice Lawes died. You've heard the evidence, or most of it. But it may be as well to emphasize it.

"Sir Maurice Lawes, on that day, went out for his afternoon walk as usual. His favorite walk, as we've heard, was through the Zoological Gardens behind the Donjon Hotel. But there's more evidence than this. On this occasion, to the surprise of waiters and barmen, he actually went so far as to come into the back bar of the hotel."

Helena turned round to peer in evident bewilderment at her brother, who was watching Dermot with a hard, wary stare. But it was Janice who answered.

"Really?" remarked Janice, lifting her round chin. "*I* hadn't heard *that* little bit of information."

"Perhaps not. Anyway, I tell you so. I questioned the people in the bar this morning. Later, he was seen in the Zoological Gardens: near, of all places, the monkey house. He appeared to be speaking to somebody, who was hidden behind a bush from the witness's view. You might remember that little incident. It is significant. It's a prelude to murder."

"Are you telling us," gulped Helena, with her wide round eyes fixed on Dermot's face, and her color rising, "that you know who killed Maurice?"

"Yes."

"And where," inquired Janice, "did you get your idea?"

"As a matter of fact, Miss Lawes, I got it from *you*."

Dermot pondered on this for a moment.

"Lady Lawes was helpful, too," he added, "by introducing the topic that you pursued. It's in the realm of the mind, actually," he rubbed his hand across his forehead, and looked apologetic, "that one little thing leads to another. However, let me go on with my story.

"Before dinner Sir Maurice returned home. He had made what the barman described as 'ferocious eyes' before even the significant meeting in the Zoological Gardens. But, by the time he returned home, he was in that white and shaky state we've so often heard described. He refused to go to the theatre. He shut himself up in his study. At eight o'clock in the evening, the rest of you set out for the theatre. Correct?"

Uncle Ben rubbed his chin.

"Yes, that's all true enough. But why repeat it again?"

"Because it's very instructive. You, together with Eve Neill, returned from the theatre about eleven o'clock. In the meantime, M. Veille the art dealer had phoned at half-past eight about his new treasure, had come with the snuff-box, and had left it. The rest of you, however, had heard nothing about any snuff-box until your return. Still correct?"

"Yes," admitted Uncle Ben.

"Certainly Eve Neill had heard nothing about a snuff-box at any time. By the testimony, which M. Goron repeated to me yesterday, she did not actually accompany you back to your house. Mr. Lawes," he nodded towards Toby, "dropped her off at her own villa, where he said good-night."

"Look here," cried Toby, with sudden wildness, "what *is* this? What are you getting at?"

"Am I still giving the evidence correctly?"

"Yes. But—"

Toby checked his gesture of impatience. While the flickering white light still played beyond, getting on their nerves even though they were not compelled to face it, there had been another knock at the door. M. Vautour rose to his feet, as did Dermot. Three persons entered the office. The first was M. Aristide Goron. The second was a gray-haired, sad-featured woman in a serge dress which vaguely suggested a uniform. The third was Eve Neill; and the gray-haired woman's hand hovered meaningly round Eve's wrist, ready to pounce if her charge attempted to run.

Eve showed no disposition to run. Nevertheless, as she saw the worn wooden armchair raked by that inexorable light, she stiffened and drew back in such a way that the wardress's hand fastened on her wrist.

"I'm not going to sit in that chair again." She spoke calmly, but with an inflexion Dermot recognized as dangerous. "You can do what you like. But I'm not going to sit in that chair again."

"It will not be necessary, madame," said M. Vautour. "Dr. Kinross, endeavor to control yourself!"

"No, no, of course it will not be necessary!" soothed M. Goron, giving her a pat on the back. "We would not hurt you, my dear. I, the old *bonhomme*, assure you of that. At the same time, doctor, I could approach with more confidence if I were certain you had no intention of plugging me in the eye."

Dermot shut his own eyes, and opened them again.

"I suppose it's my own fault," he said bitterly. "Though I hardly thought one day, less than one day, could do any damage."

Eve smiled at him.

"It hasn't done any damage, has it?" she asked. "M. Goron tells me you've done as you promised, and that I'm — well, almost out of this."

"One must not be too sure of that, madame!" said the examining magistrate, with glowering suspicion.

"One," said Dermot, "can be as smacking well sure as one likes."

Eve was as composed, once the threat of that light had been removed, as though this were not her affair at all. Taking the armchair which M. Goron pushed out for her, she nodded with formal pleasantness to Helena, Janice, and Uncle Ben. She smiled at Toby. Then she addressed Dermot.

"I knew you would." Eve stated a fact. "Even when things seemed to be going wrong, and they pounded on the table and shouted, 'Assassin, confess,'" — in spite of herself, she started to laugh, — "I knew you had some purpose in what you asked me to do. I didn't exactly doubt you. But, my God, I was frightened!"

"Yes," said Dermot, "that's the whole trouble."

"Trouble?"

"That's what's landed you in this whole mess. You trust people. They know it. And they take advantage of it. As it happens, you can trust me; but that's neither here nor there." Dermot turned round. "There's a little third-degree of my own now. It won't be very pleasant hearing for you. Shall I continue?"

XVIII

SOMEBODY'S chair scraped on the linoleum floor.

"Yes. Continue!" snapped M. Vautour.

"I was just giving an outline of events on the night of the murder. They're too important not to be stressed. Over and over, if necessary. I had got to the point where your party," Dermot looked at Toby, "returned from the theatre at eleven o'clock. You left your fiancée on her door-step, after which you joined the others. And then?"

Janice Lawes lifted puzzled eyes.

"Daddy came downstairs," she replied, "and showed us the snuff-box."

"Yes. M. Goron told me yesterday," said Dermot, "that the police took the fragments away on the day after the murder, and after a week of very painful reconstruction they were able to put it all back together again."

Toby sat up, clearing his throat and apparently catching at a gleam of hope.

"Put it together?" he repeated.

"It will not be worth much now, M. Lawes," the prefect of police warned him.

In response to Dermot's gesture, the examining magistrate again opened the drawer of his desk. Holding it gingerly, as though it might crumble to pieces in his palm, M. Vautour took out a small object which he handed to Dermot.

Sir Maurice Lawes would not have been pleased. As the white light swept across the Emperor's snuff-box, it kindled the deepness of rose agate, it flashed on the tiny diamond watch-numerals and hands, it gleamed on the gold binding and dummy winding-stem. Yet it had a dull and (if the word can be used) sticky appearance, as though everything about it were a little blurred or out of line. Dermot held it out to them, turning it over in his fingers.

"They've put it together with fish-glue," he explained. "Somebody must have gone nearly blind at the job. And it won't open now. But you saw it when it was new?"

"Yes!" returned Toby, smiting his hand on his knee. "We saw it when it was new. What about it?"

Dermot returned the snuff-box to M. Vautour.

"At shortly past eleven o'clock, Sir Maurice Lawes retired to his study. He was annoyed at the lack of enthusiasm his family had shown for his new relic. The rest of you (I think?) went to bed.

"But you, Mr. Lawes, couldn't sleep. At one o'clock in the morning you got up, went downstairs to the drawing room, and telephoned to Eve Neill."

Toby, nodding in acknowledgment, stole a sideways glance at Eve. It was an indecipherable look. It was as though Toby wanted fervently to tell her something, but hesitated in anguish and twisted his mustache, while Eve stared straight ahead.

Dermot followed that look.

"You spoke to her for some minutes on the phone. What did you talk about?"

"Eh?"

"I said, what did you talk about?"

Toby dragged his eyes back. "How the blazes should I remember? Wait: yes, I do!" He wiped a hand across his mouth. "We talked about the play we'd seen that night."

Eve smiled a little.

"It was a play about prostitution," she interposed. "Toby was afraid I might have been shocked. The subject was preying on his mind a good deal at the time, I suppose."

"Now see here," Toby flung back in an effort at quiet patience. "When we were first engaged to be married, I told you I wasn't all I should be. I told you that, didn't I? Then are you going to hold against me something I said last night when I wasn't quite myself, and spoke without thinking?"

Eve did not reply.

"Let's return to that telephone conversation," Dermot suggested. "You spoke about the play you'd seen. Anything else?"

"Blast it, does that matter?"

"Very much."

"Well — I said something about the picnic. We'd intended to go on a picnic the following day; only we didn't, naturally. Oh, and I also mentioned that Dad had just got a new trinket for his collection."

"But you didn't say what the trinket was?"

"No."

Dermot eyed him. "For the rest of it, I quote M. Goron's account to me. After this conversation, you went upstairs to bed. The time was a few minutes past one o'clock. As you went upstairs, you noticed that your father was still up, because you saw a line of light under the door of the study. Therefore you didn't disturb him. Right?"

"Right!"

"It wasn't Sir Maurice's habit to stay up quite as late as that, I believe?"

Helena cleared her throat, and answered for Toby. "No. When we say late, we don't really mean *late* as some people do. Maurice was usually in bed by twelve."

Dermot nodded.

"And you, Lady Lawes. At a quarter past one, you

yourself got up. You went to your husband's study, to ask him to come to bed and also to expostulate about the purchase of the snuff-box. You opened the study door without knocking. The chandelier lights were off: only the desk lamp burned. You saw your husband sitting there with his back to you. But, being near-sighted, you did not notice anything wrong with him until you approached and found the blood."

Tears had started to Helena's eyes. "Is this necessary?" she demanded.

"Only one thing more is very necessary," Dermot told her. "We can pass over the tragedy. We can't pass over facts.

"The police were sent for. Both Miss Lawes and Mr. Lawes tried to go across the street and rout out Mrs. Neill. They were stopped by the policeman, who told them they must wait until the commissaire arrived.

"In the meantime, what has happened? Let's turn our attention to the incomparable Yvette Latour. Yvette (she declares) is awakened by the arrival of the police and the general uproar. Yvette goes out of her room. Here is the very crux of the evidence: here's the edge of the guillotine. Yvette sees Mrs. Neill returning to the house after the murder. Yvette sees her opening the front door with a key, creeping upstairs in her stained negligée, and, subsequently, washing off blood in the bathroom. Time — about half-past one."

M. Vautour the examining magistrate held up his hand.

"One moment!" he snapped, coming round the edge of his desk. "Even with your new evidence, I do not see the direction of this."

"No?"

"No! By her own confession, this is exactly what Madame has done."

"Yes. At half past one," Dermot pointed out.

"Well! At half past one or another time! Will you explain yourself, Dr. Kinross?"

"Willingly." Dermot had been standing by the desk. He picked up the patched snuff-box, and put it down again. Then he walked over to stand in front of Toby, whom he regarded with real curiosity.

"Isn't there anything in your testimony," he asked, "that you want to change?"

Toby blinked at him. "Me? No."

"No?" said Dermot. "Won't you admit you've been telling a pack of lies, even to save the woman you claim you're in love with?"

In the background, M. Goron softly chuckled. The examining magistrate glared at him, deprecating this; instead, the examining magistrate hurried round the side of the desk, with soft little threatening steps, and came to peer at Toby from close range.

"Yes, monsieur?" M. Vautour prompted.

Toby jumped to his feet, pushing back the chair with such force on the linoleum that it clattered over on its side.

"Lies?" he said.

"After telephoning to Mrs. Neill," said Dermot, "you claim you went upstairs, passed the door of your father's study, and saw a light under it."

M. Goron intervened.

"When Dr. Kinross and I went upstairs to examine the study yesterday," the prefect told his listeners, "the doctor appeared surprised when he saw that door. At the moment, I could not understand why. Such trifles slip the mind. But I understand now. That door — if you recall it? — is a heavy door fitting so closely against the carpet that the nap of the carpet is worn every time the door moves."

He paused. His level gesture, back and forth, conjured up in their minds the movement of the door.

"To see a light under it, at any time, would have been absolutely impossible." M. Goron paused, and then added: "But it was not the only falsehood M. Lawes told."

"No," agreed the examining magistrate. "Shall we make mention of the two necklaces?"

Dermot Kinross had not their relish for the springing of a trap. He had not the stomach to enjoy putting anyone in a corner. But, at the expression on Eve's face, he nodded.

"*Then the man in the brown gloves. . .*" Eve almost screamed.

"Yes," said Dermot. "It was your fiancé, Toby Lawes."

XIX

"It's NOT a new story," continued Dermot. "He's got a little friend named Prue Latour, a sister of the helpful Yvette. Mademoiselle Prue insists on expensive presents. She was threatening to make trouble in several directions. And his salary isn't very great. That was why he decided to steal the diamond-and-turquoise necklace out of his father's collection."

"I don't believe this," said Helena, whose thin gasps could be heard like sobs.

Dermot reflected.

"Perhaps 'steal it' isn't quite the right term. He meant no real harm, as he will probably tell us when he's able to speak. He was going to substitute an imitation necklace for it, so that his father shouldn't know, and 'borrow' it as a sop for Prue until he could pay her off."

Dermot went back to the examining magistrate's desk, where he picked up the two necklaces.

"He got the imitation necklace made. . . ."

"At Paulier's in the rue de la Gloire," supplied the prefect of police. "M. Paulier is willing to identify him as the man who commissioned the necklace."

Toby did not say anything. Without looking at

any of them, he moved swiftly across the office. M. Vautour, who thought he was making for the door, called out a warning. But this was not Toby's intention. He merely wanted, in both the figurative and literal sense, to put his face in a corner. He got as far as a line of filing cases, where he stood with his back to them all.

"Last night," — Dermot held up one necklace, — "this imitation turned up in Prue's sewing-basket. It seemed worth while, before I left for London, to write a note suggesting that M. Goron might pick it up from Prue and attempt to trace it. Toby Lawes gave it to her, of course."

"To be quite frank," Eve Neill said unexpectedly, "that doesn't surprise me."

"No, madame?" demanded M. Goron.

"No! I asked him last night if he hadn't given it to her. He denied it. But he gave her a very queer look that said, 'You back up what I say!' as plainly as though he'd spoken." Suddenly Eve brushed a hand across her eyes. Her color was rising. "Prue's a practical girl. When he asked her where she'd got it, she did back him up and kept her mouth shut. But why give the woman an *imitation* necklace?"

"Because," answered Dermot, "it wasn't necessary to give her the real one."

"Not necessary?"

"No. Once Sir Maurice was dead, that fine young man thought he could always pay Prue out of his father's estate."

Helena Lawes shrieked.

This satisfied the dramatic sense of M. Goron and M. Vautour, who almost beamed at her. But it satisfied nobody else. Benjamin Phillips got up and stood behind his sister's chair, putting his hands on Helena's shoulders to steady her. Dermot now seemed to be using a whip; it was as though you could hear it hiss and crack.

"He couldn't be aware that his father was almost as hard up as he was," Dermot went on.

"It must have been quite a shock to him. Eh?" said M. Goron.

"I haven't any doubt it was. Just before the time of the murder, as Prue herself admitted last night, she was cutting up a very great row. She had been making trouble ever since the announcement of his engagement to Eve Neill. Undoubtedly, also — in her less independent moments — she had used threats like breach of promise. If she hadn't, rest assured her sister Yvette had: terrifying this gentleman with all the blanched faces at Hookson's Bank. Remember, as M. Goron will tell you, that Prue is a respectable girl.

"The necklace, he thought, should satisfy her. The real necklace, that is. After all, it must be worth a hundred thousand francs. He got his duplicate made. But still he hesitated to make the substitution."

"Why?" Eve asked calmly.

Dermot grinned at her.

"After all, you know," Dermot answered, "he *has* got a conscience."

Still Toby did not speak or turn round.

"Then he made up his mind. Whether it was because he'd just seen a particular play acted that night, or some other reason, we can ask him to tell us. But something pushed him over the edge.

"At one o'clock in the morning he spoke to his fiancée on the phone. In talking to her, he utterly convinced himself (do I read him rightly?) that his whole future happiness lay in stealing that necklace to get rid of Prue Latour. He was sincere. He was almost holy. He meant it all for the best. And this, ladies and gentlemen, is not said as sarcasm."

Dermot paused, still standing by the examining magistrate's desk.

"It would be easy. His father, at least to his knowledge, never sat up as late as this. The study should be dark and empty. All he had to do was slip in, open the curio cabinet just to the left of the door, exchange the false necklace for the real, and go on his way rejoicing.

"At a few minutes past one, then, he decided to

act. In the best detective story tradition, he put on a pair of brown work-gloves which are used by half the people in that house. The imitation necklace was already in his pocket. He slipped up the stairs. Since he was unable to see anything under the sill of the door, he naturally supposed the room would be dark and empty. But it was not dark, and it was not empty. Sir Maurice Lawes, we have heard several times, had no use for dishonesty."

"Easy, Helena!" muttered Uncle Ben.

Helena struggled out of his grip. "Are you accusing my son of murdering his father?"

And at last Toby spoke.

Over there in his self-imposed corner, the searchlight beam bringing out the tiny bald spot on the back of his head as it swung past, Toby seemed struck by a new realization. He peered round furtively. Then abruptly he appeared to think they had gone far enough with this latest nonsense, and he jumped out at them in consternation.

"*Murder*?" he repeated incredulously.

"That was the word, young man," M. Goron said.

"Now, draw it mild!" urged Toby, a hollow note of accusation in his voice. He pushed out his hands, as though he would push them away. "You didn't think I'd *killed* Dad, did you?"

"Why not?" asked Dermot.

"Why not? Why not? Kill my own father?" The dumbfounded Toby had no time even to bother with this. He took up a new grievance. "I never heard anything about these blasted 'brown gloves' until last night. Eve never mentioned them to me, until she suddenly up and sprang them on me at Prue's. Just like that!

"You could have knocked me over with a feather. I as good as told her last night, I've as good as told all of you today, that the 'brown gloves' had nothing at all to do with his death or anybody's death. Great Scott, don't you understand? *Dad was already dead when I got there!*"

"Got him!" said Dermot, and brought down his hand with a flat whack on the table.

That noise made nerves stir and tingle. Toby shied back.

"What do you mean, got him?"

"Never mind. You did wear the gloves, then?"

"Well . . . yes."

"And you found your father dead in his chair when you went in to rob him?"

Toby took another step backwards.

"I don't call it robbing him, exactly. You said so yourself. I didn't like doing it. But how else could I have got what I wanted without doing something really dishonest?"

"You know, Toby," observed Eve, in something like awe, "you're a beauty. You really are a beauty!"

"Suppose," suggested Dermot, perching himself on the edge of the desk, "we omit the ethical considerations. Just tell us what happened to you."

A genuine shudder went through Toby. If he had felt like keeping up a pretense of bravado, he could not manage it any longer. He wiped the back of his hand across his forehead.

"There isn't anything *to* tell. But you've succeeded in humiliating me in front of my mother and my sister. So I might as well get the rest of it off my chest.

"All right: I did it. Just as you said. I went up there just after I'd talked to Eve. The rest of the house was all quiet. I had the imitation necklace in the pocket of my dressing gown. I opened the door. Then I saw that the desk lamp was burning, and that the poor old governor was sitting there with his back to me.

"That's all I did see. I'm near-sighted too, you know. Like mother. You may have noticed it from the way I," — again he made one of those characteristic gestures, his hand shading his eyes, and blinked, — "never mind! I ought to wear glasses. I always do, at the bank. So I couldn't tell he was dead, either.

"First I started to close the door and duck out in a hell of a hurry. Then I thought: why not? Do you know how it is? You plan something. Then you put it off, and put it off. And at last it seems that if you *don't* get on and do it, you'll go scatty.

"That's why I thought: why not? The old governor's partly deaf, and he's all absorbed in that snuff-box. The curio cabinet's just by the door of the study. All I needed to do was reach in and change the necklaces, and who's the wiser? Then I could get some sleep and forget that little devil in the rue de la Harpe. So I reached out. The cabinet door hasn't got any lock or catch. It opens without a sound. I picked up the necklace. And then. . ."

Toby paused.

The white searchlight beam wheeled across the room, but none of the rest of them noticed it. The urgency of Toby's manner forced attention with painful intensity.

"I knocked that music box off the glass shelf," he added.

Again he searched for words.

"It's a big, heavy music box, made out of wood and tin, and it's got little wheels. It stands on the glass shelf beside the necklace. My hand struck it. It fell off on the floor with a crash fit to wake the dead. The poor old governor was rather deaf, but he wasn't deaf enough not to hear that crash.

"And that's not all. The music box no sooner hit

the floor than it started to whir, and twist as though it were alive, and then it commenced to play *John Brown's Body*. It tinkled as loud as twenty music boxes in the middle of the night, while I stood there with the necklace in my hand.

"I looked round. But the poor old governor still didn't move."

Again Toby swallowed hard.

"That was how I came to go closer, and look at him. You know what I found. I turned on the ceiling lights to make sure, but there wasn't any doubt about it. I was still holding the necklace. That must have been when I got some blood on the necklace, though I didn't get any blood on my gloves. The governor was as peaceful as sleep, except for his battered head. And all this time the music box was still playing *John Brown's Body*.

"I had to shut it up. I ran back, and picked it up, and shoved it back in the cabinet. What's more, I realized I couldn't change the necklaces now. This was something for the police. I thought a burglar'd done it. But if I gave Prue a necklace worth a hundred thousand francs, and the police heard about it, and then discovered an imitation in the cabinet. . . .

"I lost my head. Who the devil wouldn't have? I looked over, and there was a poker hanging as calm as you please among the fire irons. I went over and picked it up. There was blood and hair on it. I put it back. That finished me. All I could think of was getting out of there. I started to put the necklace back in the curio cabinet, but it slipped on the plush background (which slants upright, remember?), and fell down under the cabinet, and I let it stay there. But I had sense enough to switch off the central lights before I left. That seemed only decent, somehow."

His voice trailed away.

The examining magistrate's office was full of evil images.

Dermot Kinross, sitting on the edge of M. Vautour's desk, studied Toby with an expression in which it was hard to separate the cynicism from the admiration.

"You never mentioned this to anybody?" he asked.

"No."

"Why not?"

"I — it might have been misunderstood. People mightn't have understood my motives."

"I see. Any more than they understood Eve Neill's motives, when she told *her* story? Then can you, in fairness, ask us to believe in yours?"

"Stop it!" begged Toby. "How was I to know anybody saw anything from that blasted window across the street?" He glanced at Eve. "First off,

Eve herself swore she hadn't seen anything. I appeal to all of you if that's not so! I never heard anything about these 'brown gloves' until last night."

"Yet you never told about this escapade of yours, even though it must have done so much to show your fiancée was innocent?"

Toby looked dazed. "I don't follow that!"

"No? Look here. Immediately after you telephoned to her at one o'clock, you went upstairs and found your father dead?"

"Yes."

"Therefore, if she killed him, she did it before one o'clock? At one o'clock — her work finished — she is back in her bedroom talking to you?"

"Yes."

"Her work is finished and she is back home by one o'clock. Then how is it that she goes out of the house *again*, and doesn't come back until one-thirty, with fresh blood on her?"

Toby opened his mouth, and shut it again.

"It won't do, you know," Dermot objected with deceptive mildness. "Twice is too much. This whole scene described by Yvette, of the terrified murderess creeping back from her crime at half-past one, unlocking the front door, 'much tousled,' and hastening to wash the blood from herself: no. It's too much of a good thing. You don't suggest she went out and committed *another* murder, after Sir Maurice Lawes had been dead for half an hour? Because, being back home following the death of her first victim, she must surely have tidied herself up before going out again?"

Dermot, his arms folded, lounged idly on the edge of the desk.

"You agree, M. Vautour?" he inquired.

Helena Lawes shook herself free from her brother's restraining grasp.

"I can't understand these subtleties," Helena said. "All I'm interested in is my son."

"Well, I'm not," interposed Janice unexpectedly. "If Toby's been carrying on with that girl in the rue de la Harpe, and Toby did what he admits he did, I say we've been treating Eve in a filthy way."

"Be quiet, Janice. *If* Toby did that, as you say. . ."

"Mother, he admits it!"

"Then I daresay he had a good reason. With all due respect to Eve, and I'm only too glad if she can get out of this, that's not what I'm concerned with. Dr. Kinross, is *Toby* telling the truth?"

"Oh, yes," said Dermot.

"He didn't kill poor Maurice?"

"Certainly not."

"But somebody did," Uncle Ben pointed out. Uncle Ben's eyes shifted.

"Yes. Somebody did," acknowledged Dermot. "We were coming to that."

Throughout this, the only person who had not spoken was Eve herself. While the white light swung, flinging distorted shadows of these people on the walls — a moving procession like a shadow show — Eve had sat staring at the tips of her shoes. Only once, at a certain part of the recital, did she hold tightly to the arms of her chair as though recalling something. There were faint shadows under her eyes, and the white mark of her teeth in her lower lip. She nodded to herself. Now she looked up, meeting Dermot's eye.

"I think I've remembered," she told him, clearing her throat, "what you wanted me to remember."

"I owe you an explanation. Also an apology."

"No!" said Eve. "No, no, no! I understand now why I got into trouble when I told my story today."

"Well, if you'll let me speak without shushing me," protested Janice, "*I* don't understand it. What's the answer?"

"The answer," replied Dermot, "is the name of the murderer."

"Ah!" murmured M. Goron.

Eve contemplated the Emperor's snuff-box, glowing with all its colors on the desk beside Dermot's hand.

"I've been nine days in a nightmare," she went on. "A nightmare of brown gloves. I couldn't think of anything else. And then they turn out to be only Toby."

"Thanks," muttered the gentleman in question.

"I wasn't being sarcastic. I mean it. If you're so concentrated on a thing like that, you don't consciously remember other things. Also, you're ready to swear something is true which really isn't **true**. You think it is, but it isn't. It's only sometimes, when you're so exhausted that your conscious brain doesn't work, you remember the truth."

Helena Lawes's voice had gone high.

"Really, my dear," she cried, "this may be all very psychological and Freudian and what not, but will you please tell us what in the name of heaven you're talking about?"

"That snuff-box," answered Eve.

"What about it?"

"It was smashed by one of the murderer's blows. Just afterwards, the police gathered up all the fragments and took them away to fit them together. Do you know, this is the first time in my life I've ever set eyes on it."

"But —!" began Janice in evident bewilderment.

Dermot Kinross pointed.

"Look at the snuff-box," he suggested. "It's not

large. Two and a quarter inches across, according to the measurements Sir Maurice wrote down. And what does it look like, even seen close at hand? It looks exactly like a watch. In fact, when Sir Maurice first showed it to his family, they thought it *was* a watch. Is that right?"

"Yes," admitted Uncle Ben. "But . . ."

"It certainly doesn't suggest a snuff-box in any way?"

"No."

"It was never, at any time previous to the murder, shown to Eve Neill or described to her?"

"Apparently not."

"Then how, when she declares she saw it from a distance of fifty feet away, could she have known it was a snuff-box?"

Eve closed her eyes.

M. Goron and the examining magistrate exchanged glances.

"That's the whole answer," continued Dermot. "That, and the power of suggestion."

"Power of suggestion?" screamed Helena.

"The murder in this case has been very clever. A damnably brilliant plot, with Eve Neill as its second victim, was constructed to provide the criminal with a cast-iron alibi for the murder of Sir Maurice Lawes. And he very nearly got away with it.

Would you like to know who the murderer is?"

Dermot slid off the edge of the desk. He walked to the door giving on the hall, and flung the door open as the white beam from the searchlight circled again.

"In fact, he's been egomaniac enough to insist on coming here, in spite of our efforts to prevent him, and testify for himself. Come in, my friend. You're very welcome."

Clear in the bluish-white glare, they saw just outside the white, staring face of Ned Atwood.

XX

In late afternoon of a fine day just a week later, Janice Lawes voiced her views.

"Then the blameless witness of the crime, whose lips were sealed because he couldn't compromise a lady's reputation," Janice said, "was actually the man who committed the crime? Isn't that something new?"

"Ned Atwood thought it was," Dermot admitted. "He took the case of Lord William Russell, at London in 1840, and he put a reverse twist on it.

"His object, as I told you, was to provide himself with an alibi for the murder of Sir Maurice. Eve was to be his alibi and his witness: all the more convincing because she would be an *unwilling* witness, do you see?"

Eve shivered.

"That was the original scheme, which I'll explain to you. Ned couldn't know that Toby Lawes would walk smack into the middle of it, wearing a pair of brown gloves: thus providing him with a victim as well as a witness. When Atwood saw that, he must have shouted and thought it was too good to be true. On the other hand, he couldn't have foreseen that

272

he would fall downstairs and get concussion of the brain: thus, as it eventually happened, ruining his whole plan. So the honors of chance are even on both sides."

"Come on," Eve said abruptly. "Let's hear about it, please. *All* about it."

A slight tension gathered round them. Eve, Dermot, Janice, and Uncle Ben were sitting after tea in the back garden of Eve's villa, in the shade of the high walls and chestnut trees. The table had been set out under a tree, whose leaves were now touched with faint traces of yellow.

(The autumn is coming, thought Dermot Kinross, and I go back to London tomorrow).

"Yes," he said. "I want to tell you about it. Vautour and Goron and I have been gathering up the threads all week."

Looking at Eve's anxious face, he bitterly hated what he had to tell.

"You've been infernally close-mouthed," grumbled Uncle Ben. After an uneasy whir in the throat, he burst out: "What still beats me is the fellow's motive for killing Maurice!"

"And me," said Eve. "What was it? He didn't even *know* Papa Lawes, did he?"

"Not consciously," answered Dermot.

"What do you mean, not consciously?"

Dermot leaned back in the wicker-chair, crossing his knees. When he lit one of his Maryland cigarettes, the concentration of his expression — an angry concentration — made more lines appear in the face than were customarily there. But he tried not to show this when he smiled at Eve.

"I want you to think back over several matters we've discovered. When you were still married to Atwood, and living here in the old days," — he saw her flinch, — "you weren't yet acquainted with the Lawes family, were you?"

"No."

"But you several times noticed the old man?"

"Yes, that's right."

"And, whenever he saw you and Atwood together, he looked very hard at you two, as though perplexed? Yes. He was trying to remember where he had seen Ned Atwood before."

Eve sat up. A sudden premonition, an inspired guess, flashed through her mind. But Dermot was not guessing.

"And once," he went on, "after you were engaged to Toby Lawes, Sir Maurice started to question you about Atwood in a veiled way; but hemm'd and haw'd, and gave you an odd look and said nothing else? Yes. Now, you married Atwood. But what do you know about him, even now? What did you ever learn about him: his previous history, background, anything?"

Eve moistened her lips.

"Nothing at all! Oddly enough, I was throwing that at him on the very night of — the murder."

Dermot next looked at Janice, who had also opened her mouth with an expression of startled and dawning comprehension.

"You told me, my girl, that your father had a very bad memory for faces. But, every once in a while, something would remind him with a bang and he'd remember where he had seen a certain person before. Well, he had seen many faces, naturally, in the course of his prison work. We're not likely to learn just *when* he remembered *where* he'd seen Atwood before. What he did remember was that 'Atwood,' a model convict, had escaped from prison while serving a five years' sentence at Wandsworth for bigamy."

"*Bigamy?*" cried Eve.

But she did not contradict. In imagination she saw Ned stepping across the twilight grass, as clearly as though she could see him in the flesh, and watch his grin.

"A Patrick-Mahon sort of fellow," Dermot went on. "Very attractive to women. A Continental drifter, keeping away from England. Picking up money here and there on a business deal, but also borrowing from —" Dermot checked himself.

"Anyhow, you can see the shape of events take form.

"You and Atwood were divorced. I can't exactly say that: legally, you were never married. And his name, by the way, isn't Atwood. You must have a look at his record one day. After the so-called divorce, Atwood went to the United States. He said he was going to get you back, and he meant to do so. But, in the meantime, you became engaged to Toby Lawes.

"Sir Maurice was well satisfied. In fact, he was delighted. He meant to let nothing, *nothing*, stand in the way of this match. I know Janice and Mr. Phillips will understand what I mean when I say. . ."

There was a silence.

"Yes," grunted Uncle Ben, chewing at his pipe. He added fiercely: "Always been on Eve's side myself."

Janice looked at Eve.

"I treated you rottenly," she burst out, "because I didn't understand what a selfish swine Toby is. Yes, I say that: even if he is my brother! But, as far as you were concerned, I never really thought. . ."

"Not even," smiled Dermot, "when you suggested she might have been in prison?"

Janice put out her tongue at him.

"But you gave us the clue," Dermot went on. "In essentials, you gave us the whole story in that parable about the man called Finisterre or McConklin. For notice what happened! History repeated itself. You can't be blamed if you had it the wrong way round. Now, I think it was well known all over the place that Ned Atwood had returned to La Bandelette, and was putting up at the Donjon.

"Sir Maurice went out for his afternoon walk. Where did he go? To the back bar of the Donjon Hotel. And who, as we've known all along, was in that bar? Ned Atwood, loudly boasting he was going to get his wife back, no matter what he had to tell people about her.

"You, Janice, even suggested once that Atwood met your father, and talked to him. That's exactly what happened. Your father said, 'Will you come outside and have a word with me, sir?' Atwood didn't know what was up. But he went. And he learned — with what sick rage we can imagine — that the old man was very well posted about *his* history.

"They walked in the Zoological Gardens. Sir Maurice, trembling a good deal, said exactly what he once said to Finisterre. Do you remember?"

Janice nodded.

" '*I'll give you twenty-four hours to make your-*

self scarce,'" Janice quoted. "'*At the end of that time, whether you've done it or not, a full account of you in your new life — where you're to be found — your new name — everything about you — goes to Scotland Yard.*'"

Again Dermot, who had been bending forward, leaned back in the wicker chair.

"This is catastrophe coming out of nowhere. Atwood won't get his wife back now, as he's firmly convinced he can do. He won't have his soft life any longer. No: he'll go back to prison. If you can imagine him roaming through those gardens, past the cages of wild beasts, you can imagine something of what went on in his mind. Out of the blue, a monstrous injustice, he'll be taken back to prison.

"Unless . . .

"He didn't know Sir Maurice Lawes in the sense of being acquainted with him. But he knew quite a lot about the habits of the household at the Villa Bonheur. Remember, he lived here for several years.

"He had seen for himself that Sir Maurice, after the rest of the family had retired, was in the habit of sitting up alone in the study. From across the street he had seen into the study many times, just as Eve herself had. He knew the lay-out of the study, whose curtains were not closed in warm weather. He knew where Sir Maurice sat, where the door was, where the fire irons hung. Best of all, he had in his possession a key to the front door of Eve's house which — remember? — *also fitted the front door of the Villa Bonheur.*"

Benjamin Phillips meditatively scratched his forehead with the stem of his pipe.

"I say. Evidence can point both ways, can't it?"

"It can. It does." Dermot hesitated. "The next part won't be pleasant hearing for any of you. Do you honestly want it?"

"Go on!" cried Eve.

"If he acted, he had to act at once to shut Sir Maurice's mouth forever. He reasoned, rightly, that Sir Maurice wouldn't mention this to anybody until Atwood had 'got out of town,' if only to avoid an open scandal. But, even so, he must have an iron-clad alibi to protect him in the event of a slip. While he walked in the garden, his cleverness and his conceit worked out the plan of the alibi in ten minutes. You will see in a moment what it was.

"He knew everybody's grooves of habit. He was hanging about the rue des Anges when your party returned from the theatre. Eve went to her villa, the rest of you to yours. He waited patiently until the rest of you had retired; until all your lights were out, except the light in those uncurtained study windows.

He didn't mind the open curtains. They formed a part of his scheme."

Though Janice was white to the lips, she could not help asking a question.

"What about the danger of being seen from one of the houses across the street?"

"Which house across the street?" asked Dermot.

"I — I see," said Eve. "*My* curtains are always drawn. And the villas on either side are unoccupied, as late in the season as this."

"Yes," said Dermot. "So Goron told me. We return to the ingenious Mr. Atwood. He was ready to act. Using his key, he opened the front door of Sir Maurice's house. . . ."

"At what time?"

"At about twenty minutes to one."

Dermot's cigarette had burnt itself to a yellowing stump. He dropped it on the ground, and set his heel on it.

"My guess is that he had brought along some weapon to use, some equally silent weapon, in case there was no poker among the fire irons. But he needn't have worried. The poker was there. From what he later told Eve herself, we know that he was aware of Sir Maurice's deafness. He opened the door, caught up the poker, and approached his victim from behind. There sat the old man, immersed in a study of the new treasure. A writing pad in front of him bore, in very large ornamental letters, the words 'SNUFF-BOX, shaped like a watch.'

"The murderer lifted his arm, and struck. Once having struck, he went berserk."

In imagination Eve, who knew Ned Atwood, saw the thing done.

"One of the blows, perhaps by accident but more probably by design, smashed the costly-looking trinket. Atwood must have wondered what he had broken. Staring up at him, always, were those large words 'SNUFF-BOX,' — the first words would undoubtedly strike his eye, — from a stained but legible writing pad. They made a deep impression on him, as we shall see. And now for the most important part!"

Dermot turned to Eve.

"What sort of suit was Atwood wearing that night?"

"A — a fuzzy, roughish kind of dark suit. I don't know what the material's called."

"Yes," agreed Dermot. "That's it. When he smashed the snuff-box, a tiny chip of it flew wide and caught in his coat. He never noticed it. Later, it was accidentally transferred to your white lace negligée when he put his arms round you during that episode in the bedroom.

"You never noticed it either. In fact, you were willing to swear it had never been there, and to think in all honesty that somebody must have planted it on you. But the truth is much simpler. That's all there is to it." He looked at Janice and Uncle Ben. "I hope the sinister chip of agate does not seem quite so mysterious now?

"But I am getting ahead of myself. I have been telling you this as we later reconstructed it, not as the case first presented itself to me. When Goron first told me about it, it seemed more than probable that the murderer must have been a member of the Lawes family. You can't resent that, because you've thought of it yourselves.

"I was puzzled a little by certain circumstances in Eve's first, very brief recital to Goron at the Villa Bonheur that first afternoon. But it wasn't until late the same night — when she told me her full story over omelettes at Papa Rousse's — that my wits woke up out of stupor, and the ghost of an idea took shape, and I realized we had been looking in the wrong direction. *You* understand that part of it now."

Eve shivered.

"Yes. I understand it only too well."

"For clearness to these people here, let's reconstruct. Atwood arrived at your house at a quarter to one, letting himself in with that invaluable key. . . ."

"He was practically glassy-eyed," cried Eve, "and I thought he'd been drinking. What's more, he was under some kind of mental strain and almost in tears. I'd never seen Ned quite like that before. It scared me. It was worse than any of his drinking-bouts. But he hadn't been drinking."

"No," said Dermot. "He had just come from killing a man. Killing a man like that was a little too much even for Ned Atwood's self-assurance. He had left the Villa Bonheur, slipped away to the Boulevard du Casino, loitered there a minute or two, and then returned to the opposite villa as though he were entering the street for the first time. He was now all ready to prepare his alibi.

"But never mind that. Take only the evidence as we've seen it. He burst in on you. He began to talk about the Lawes family, and the old man sitting across the street. Finally, having reduced you to a state of wild nerves, he pulled back the window-curtain and started to look out. You switched off the light. Now! Repeat to me again, verbatim, what you two said during the next minute."

Eve closed her eyes.

"I said, *'Is Maurice Lawes still up? Is he?'*

"Ned said, *'Yes, he's still up. But he's not paying any attention. He's got a magnifying glass, and he's looking at some kind of snuff-box thing. — Hold on!'*

"I said, '*What is it?*'

"Ned said, '*There's somebody with him, but I can't see who it is.*'

"I said, '*Toby, probably. Ned Atwood, will you come away from that window?*'"

Drawing a deep breath, feeling only too clearly the recollection of that hot dim bedroom in the night quiet, Eve opened her eyes.

"That's all," she added.

"But did you yourself," insisted Dermot, "look out of the window at any time?"

"No."

"No; you took his word for it." Dermot turned to the others. "Now the startling thing there, the surprise like a blow in the face, was what Atwood claimed to have seen. If he saw anything at all, he saw from fifty feet away a small object which looked exactly like a watch. Yet he sang out unhesitatingly and called it a "snuff-box thing." In fact, this clever gentleman gave himself away. He couldn't have known that. He couldn't have known it, that is, unless there was a very sinister explanation of why he knew it.

"But notice what he does next!

"Instantly he starts in attempting to convince Eve that *she* has looked out of the window with him, — that she has seen Sir Maurice alive and well, holding a magnifying glass, with a sinister shadow hovering over him.

"He does it by suggestion. He does it repeatedly, as you could see if you had a transcript of the evidence before you. It is always, 'Do you remember what *we* saw?' Here is a woman very susceptible to the power of suggestion, as a brother psychologist once told her and as I noted for myself. Her nerves are unstrung; she is ready to see anything. Then, once the impression is there, the curtains on the window are swept aside and she is shown Sir Maurice's dead body.

"That was where I woke up.

"The whole purpose of this game was to convince her she had seen something which she had not seen: that is, Sir Maurice alive while Atwood was with her.

"Atwood was the murderer. This was his plan. And, except for one thing, it would have succeeded. He did convince her. She quite sincerely believed she had seen Sir Maurice alive in his study, as she had seen him on so many other nights, in the same posture. She told Goron so at their first interview in my presence. If the snuff-box had been an ordinary snuff-box, and had looked like one, this very intelligent Mr. Atwood would have got away with it."

Dermot brooded, his elbow on the arm of the chair, and his chin on his fist.

"Dr. Kinross," Janice observed softly, "that's rather clever."

"Clever? Of course he was clever! The fellow obviously knew the history of crime backwards. He was so quick to drag in the Lord William Russell case that anybody must have suspected. . ."

"No: I mean your reading of it."

Dermot laughed. He was not very proud of himself at the best of times, and his laughter had a wryness which affected his throat like bitter medicine.

"That? Anybody could have seen that. There are certain women who seem born to be — victimized by swine.

"For now you can see all the cross-currents which confused us. Toby Lawes blundered into the plan, wearing brown gloves. It was manna from heaven. Atwood was both astounded and delighted, if Eve has described his behavior correctly to me. It provided the last realistic touch which made him safe.

"You see now what the end of his game was to be? He never intended to figure publicly in the business at all, if he could help it. He must keep out of the way. There was, on the surface, nothing to connect him with Sir Maurice. The less said about that, the better. But, in the event of any slip-up, there was his alibi all prepared: ready to be dragged out of an unwilling woman, over whom he was convinced he had complete ascendancy, and all the more convincing an alibi because it was a discreditable one.

"That, of course, was why he told the story about being 'hit by a car' when he collapsed at the hotel later. He wasn't going to mention the matter at all, unless he had to. And he never for an instant imagined he was badly hurt.

"But that was what upset his whole plan. First, he was accidentally pushed into a fall that gave him concussion of the brain. Second, the vindictive Yvette intervened, with a game of her own to play. Atwood, naturally, never intended to have any suspicion whatever directed towards Eve. It was the last thing he ever could have anticipated. While he lay unconscious with concussion, he would have been horrified to learn what was going on."

"Then it really *was* Yvette," Janice interrupted, "who slammed the door and locked Eve out of the house?"

"Oh, yes. About Yvette, we can only guess. She is a Norman peasant; she refuses to say anything; and all Vautour's efforts can't beat a word out of her. It seems likely that she knew nothing about the murder when she locked Eve out. She knew Atwood was there. And she was trying to create a scandal, so that your pious brother would perhaps break off the marriage.

"But Yvette, I repeat, is a Norman peasant. When

she saw to her own astonishment that Eve Neill had become involved in a suspicion of murder, she never hesitated and never lost face. She joined in the prosecution with zeal. She pushed *that* charge for all it was worth. It was an even better way of breaking off the marriage. She had no concern with right or wrong; her concern was to get her sister Prue married to Toby.

"This was the state of mix-up, then, on the night when I visited the rue de la Harpe, found the two necklaces, and heard Eve's full story — which showed who the murderer was. Once you had grasped that, it wasn't difficult to think back. It wasn't difficult to fit in the other pieces of evidence.

"The question was: what was Atwood's motive for murder? The answer clearly lay in Sir Maurice's prison work, described by his wife and daughter, and elaborated by that little story about Finisterre. Could I verify my theory? Easily! If Atwood were wanted by the police, or even if he had ever committed a crime at all under any name, his fingerprints would be on file in the Records Department at Scotland Yard."

Uncle Ben whistled.

"Oh, ah!" he muttered, and sat up. "Got it! That flying trip of yours to London . . . ?"

"We couldn't move until I knew. I got Atwood's

prints, unnoticed, by visiting his room at the hotel, taking his pulse, and pressing his fingers on the silver back of my watch. It seemed appropriate to use a watch. And, God knows, the duplicates of those prints were easily found in the Records Department. In the meantime . . ."

"The apple-cart had been upset again," supplied Eve, and began to laugh in spite of herself.

"They arrested you, yes," said Dermot. His face darkened. "But I can't see, even yet, that it was so very damned funny."

He turned to the others.

"When she gave me the account in detail, she was so tired that her inner mind — the subconscious we all make so much fun of — spoke out and told a truth she wasn't aware of herself. She hadn't actually looked out of the window with Atwood and seen Sir Maurice alive, as it was easy to deduce from the very words she spoke. She had never even set eyes on the snuff-box. It was Atwood who put the words into her mouth.

"I couldn't joggle her memory or try to start counter-suggestions. What she said was just what I wanted. It showed Atwood's guilt as plain as print. I told her to tell her story to Goron exactly as she had told it to me. Once that was on the record, and I could get my proof of Atwood's motive to back it up, it would be possible to go ahead and explain my case.

"But I hadn't allowed for the strength of Atwood's suggestion in her mind, or Goron and Vautour's Gallic energy. In speaking to them, she told Atwood's story and didn't give the words verbatim. . . ."

Eve protested:

"I couldn't help it! They — they kept a light on me, and kept dancing about like jumping-jacks. And you weren't there to lend moral support. . . ."

A curious expression crossed Janice's face as she looked first at Eve and then at Dermot. Both of them showed a sharp, momentary, almost angry confusion.

"Consequently," Dermot rushed on, "they woke up. Only they took *Atwood's* slip and applied it to *her.* Oho? Nobody has ever told her anything about Sir Maurice's new treasure, eh? She hasn't heard it described? No, certainly not. Then how does she know that the watch is really a snuff-box? After that, every word of attempted explanation sounded like guilt. She was haled off to chokey with all horns blowing; and I arrived just in time to figure as the villain of the piece myself."

"I see," said Uncle Ben. "First bad luck down, then good luck up. Like a ruddy pendulum. Because Atwood recovered consciousness."

"Yes," said Dermot grimly, "Atwood recovered consciousness."

There was a vertical line between his eyebrows, pinched together at ugly memory.

"He was eager to testify that Toby was the man in the brown gloves, and complete our case. Very eager! It meant, at one stroke, getting his wife back as he planned, and sending his rival to prison. You wouldn't have thought, would you, that a fellow with an injury like that could get up out of bed, dress himself, and go across town to see Vautour? But he did. He insisted on it."

"And you didn't stop him?"

"No," said Dermot, "I didn't stop him."

After a pause Dermot went on:

"He died in the doorway of Vatour's office. He collapsed, and fell down in the passage and died, before the turn of the searchlight had time to leave him. He died of being discovered."

The sun had gone at the turn of the afternoon. The garden, where a few birds bickered, was turning cool.

"And our noble Toby . . ." began Janice. She paused, and showed a flush of anger when Dermot laughed.

"I don't think you understand your brother."

"Of all the swinish tricks I ever heard of in my life — !"

"He's not in any sense a swine. He's a perfectly

ordinary case (if you'll excuse my saying so) of arrested development."

"Meaning?"

"Mentally and emotionally, he's still fifteen years old. That's all. He honestly can't see that it could be a crime to steal from his own father. His ideas of sexual morality might have come straight from the fourth form of his old school.

"There are plenty of Tobys in this world. Often they get on well enough. They're looked on as rocks of staunchness, models of solidity, until a real crisis comes along: then the schoolboy-man without imagination or nerves goes to pieces. He's a good fellow to play golf or have a drink with. But I doubt whether he'd make the best possible husband for . . . well, leave it at that."

"I wondered —" Uncle Ben began, and stopped.

"Yes?"

"I was worried. When Maurice came back from that walk of his — all upset, shaking, that sort of thing — he spoke to Toby. He didn't say anything about Atwood, did he?"

"No," answered Janice. "I thought of that too. That's why I thought he may have found out something about *Toby*, do you see? I asked Toby, after we'd heard everything. All Daddy said was, 'I've seen somebody today, son,' meaning Atwood, evi-

dently, 'and I'll talk to you about it later.' Toby
was petrified. He thought Prue Latour was starting
to make real trouble. So he went clean up in
the air and decided to pinch the necklace that
night."

Janice moved her neck in discomfort. She added
abruptly:

"Mother's over there now," — she nodded in the
direction of the villa across the street, — "condoling
with Toby. Toby's been so very badly treated. But
then I expect all mothers are like that."

"Ah!" said Uncle Ben profoundly.

Janice got up from her chair.

"Eve," she cried with a startling vehemence, "I
was almost as bad as Toby was. But I'm sorry. Please
believe that! I'm sorry about *everything!*"

And, after struggling without effect to say something else, she ran across the garden, up the path
past the side of the villa, and disappeared. Uncle Ben
rose more slowly.

"Don't go!" said Eve. "Don't —"

Uncle Ben paid no attention to this. He was pon-
dering deeply.

"I'm not," he grunted. "Sorry, I mean. Good thing
for you, if you know what I mean. You and Toby.
No." Powerfully embarrassed, he turned away, but
swung back again. "I made you a ship-model this

week," he added. "Thought you might like it. I'll
send it over when it's painted. G'bye."

And he shambled away.

When he had gone, Eve Neill and Dr. Dermot
Kinross sat silent for a long time. They did not look
at each other. It was Eve who spoke first.

"Was it true what you said yesterday?"

"About what?"

"About having to go back to London tomorrow?"

"Yes. I've got to get back sooner or later. The point
is, what are *you* going to do?"

"I don't know. Dermot: I wanted to —"

He interrupted her. "Now, look here. Any more
of this damned gratitude —"

"Well, you needn't be so snappish about it!"

"I was not being snappish about it. I was only
trying to get gratitude out of your mind."

"Why? Why have you done all this for me?"

Dermot picked up the packet of Maryland cigarettes. He offered it to her, but she shook her head.
He lit one himself.

"That's an infantile trick," he said. "You know
perfectly well. One day, when you're over this state
of nerves, we may talk about it again. In the meantime, I still ask what you're going to do?"

Eve shrugged her shoulders.

"I don't know. I thought of packing my traps and

going down to Nice or Cannes for a while...."

"You can't do that."

"Why not?"

"Because it's impossible. Our friend Goron was quite right in what he said about you."

"Oh? What did he say about me?"

"He said you're a public menace, and that nobody can tell what you'll get into next. If you go to the Riviera, some prowling male or other will cross your path, make you think you're in love with him, and ... well, here we go again. No: you'd better come back to England. You won't be out of danger there, God knows; but at least an eye can be kept on you."

Eve considered this.

"As a matter of fact, I *had* thought of going to England." She lifted her eyes. "Tell me. Do you think I'm breaking my heart about Ned Atwood?"

Dermot took the cigarette out of his mouth. His eyes narrowed. He stared back at her for a long time, and then struck his fist on the arm of the chair.

"That's practical psychology," he said. "Trust *you* to go straight through verbiage, if you like."

"Do you?"

"I didn't exactly murder the fellow. 'Thou shalt not kill, but needst not strive, officiously to keep alive.' I encouraged him to die, at least. If I hadn't done it, and he'd been nursed back to health, the guillotine would have done it very efficiently. But I wasn't considering that side of it."

Dermot's face darkened.

"Toby Lawes," he went on, "was never anything to you. You were lonely and you were bored and you wanted somebody to rely on. You mustn't ever make *that* mistake again, and I'm going to see to it you don't. If a little thing like a murder hadn't interrupted it, something else would have. But Atwood — maybe! — was different."

"Was he?"

"That fellow really loved you, in his own way. When he talked about what he thought, I doubt whether he was acting. It wouldn't prevent him from using you for his alibi. . . ."

"No. I noticed that.'

"But it didn't alter his feelings. What I wondered was whether it had altered yours. The Atwoods of this world are a little too dangerous in every sense."

Eve sat motionless. Her eyes were shining damply in the darkening garden.

"I don't mind your doing the thinking for both of us," she told him. "In fact, I prefer it. But if there's one thing I *won't* have you thinking, it's what the Lawes family thought. Will you come here for a moment, please?"

* * * * *

M. Aristide Goron, prefect of police of La Bandel-ette, swung along the rue des Anges at the stumpy but magnificent walk suggestive of the Grand Monarch. His chest was thrown out, he twirled a malacca stick, and he was well satisfied with all the world.

The learned Docteur Kinross, he had been told, would be found taking tea with Madame Neill in the back garden of the latter's villa. He, Aristide Goron, was in a position to inform both of them that the Lawes affair was now satisfactorily closed.

M. Goron beamed on the rue des Anges. This Lawes affair had redounded to the credit of the La Bandelette police department. Reporters, and especially photographers, had come from as far as Paris concerning it. He had been puzzled by Dr. Kinross's refusal to have his name concerned in the case, and in particular to being photographed. But if somebody must have the credit . . . *enfin*, let's not disappoint the public.

In fact, M. Goron had to revise his earlier suspicion about Dr. Kinross. This man was a thinking-machine, no more and no less. He was admirable. He lived for his little mental puzzles, and nothing else, exactly as he had told the prefect. He dissected minds like clocks, and was a clock himself.

M. Goron opened the gate in the wall round the Villa Miramar. Seeing, at his left, the path which led round the side of the house, he followed it.

It was a relief, too, to find some of the English who were not hypocrites like this M. Lawes. M. Goron was beginning to understand the English better now. In fact. . .

Cutting at the grass with his stick, M. Goron emerged jauntily into the back garden. The evening light was darkening; a hush was on the chestnut trees. He was just rehearsing the speech he would deliver, when he caught sight of two persons in front of him.

M. Goron stopped short.

His eyes bulged almost out of their sockets.

For a moment he stood staring. He was a discreet man, a polite man, a man who liked to see people have a good time. So he turned round, and retraced his steps. But he was also a fair-minded man, who liked to be dealt with fairly. As he emerged again in the rue des Anges, he shook his head despondently. He stumped back along the street more rapidly than he had come. He spoke in too low a voice for anybody to hear what he was muttering to himself, but the word "zizipompom" floated out and died away in the evening air.

THE END.

M8253-TN
9